I COULD NEVER FORGET ABOUT YOU

a novel by

Leslie Jane Linder

I COULD NEVER FORGET ABOUT YOU 2

a novel by 2

Leslie Jane Linder 2

PROLOGUE 12

A Long Time Ago in Mexico 12

CHAPTER 1 16

About 25 Years Ago in Florida 16

CHAPTER 2 20

I'm Still in a Fog 20

CHAPTER 3 23

I Like It Here 23

CHAPTER 4 28

Sometimes They Leave Presents 28

CHAPTER 5 32

A Boy Scout 32

CHAPTER 6 39
She Probably Already Made Bail 39

CHAPTER 7 46
What Is Your Emergency? 46

CHAPTER 8 53
Emil and Carmella 53

CHAPTER 9 60
I Just Hate Being by Myself 60

CHAPTER 10 66
Across Alligator Alley 66

CHAPTER 11 68
I'm Not Panicking 68

CHAPTER 12 71
Time For a Change 71

CHAPTER 13 74
Not If I Can Help It 74

CHAPTER 14 78
I Need to Know You're Going to Be Safe 78

CHAPTER 15 84
After Mexico 84

CHAPTER 16 86
A Terrier with An Old Sock 86

CHAPTER 17 89
What Is He Up To? 89

CHAPTER 18 93
We Can't Change the Past 93

CHAPTER 19 97
Why The Flex Cuffs? 97

CHAPTER 20 103
Not This Guy 103

CHAPTER 21 107
Lock Your Doors 107

CHAPTER 22 ... 112
Sunday Morning ... 112

CHAPTER 23 ... 113
Her Name Is Catherine ... 113

CHAPTER 24 ... 118
It Was a Long Time Ago ... 118

CHAPTER 25 ... 120
When They'd All Been Younger ... 120

CHAPTER 26 ... 125
Charlie Has a Girl ... 125

CHAPTER 27 ... 130
No Magic Like That Exists ... 130

CHAPTER 28 ... 133
A Bridal Suite ... 133

CHAPTER 29 ... 136
Second Thoughts ... 136

CHAPTER 30 141
Joel Makes the Paper 141

CHAPTER 31 145
Carmela and Emil 145

CHAPTER 32 148
Joel and Catherine and Charlie 148

CHAPTER 33 152
Might As Well Be Real About What We're Doing 152

CHAPTER 34 156
I'm Nothing If Not Flexible 156

CHAPTER 35 161
How Did He Even Find You? 161

CHAPTER 36 164
Down Time 164

CHAPTER 37 169
A Visit with Charlie's Mother 169

CHAPTER 38 174
I Need to Tell You Something 174

CHAPTER 39 180
Kill The Cop. Kill Someone..180

CHAPTER 40 182
Carmella and Joel and Charlie and Catherine 182

CHAPTER 41 188
When Was the Last Time? 188

CHAPTER 42 196
Is That a Crime?...196

CHAPTER 43 199
You Made Me Do This 199

CHAPTER 44 205
Charlie's Fantasy Life 205

CHAPTER 45 212
She's All Mine, Now...212

CHAPTER 46	216
I Told You They'd Come Someday	216

CHAPTER 47	219
Safe and Secure	219
Acknowledgments	221
Copyright	222

Epigraph

The past is never where you think you left it.

—Katherine Anne Porter

Prologue
A Long Time Ago in Mexico

Beneath the surface of the tropical ocean, her breaths were coming too fast and too shallow. She was forcing out a torrent of bubbles. Her eyes behind her mask were fixed anxiously, not really seeing anything around her. The Mexican dive guide took her arm and made eye contact. He gestured reassuringly, making a lazy circle with his hand and miming long, easy exhales and inhales. She managed to slow the pace of her breathing and became calmer by degrees. Together they continued their descent as the current carried them past towering reef formations. Joel followed, floating within the swarms of fish.

The divers glided along the Santa Rosa wall at a depth of about sixty feet. Tiki, the guide, pointed to a pod of eagle rays with five-foot wingspans flapping along languidly with the current. Schools of shimmering tropical fish streamed through the divers' columns of bubbles. The sunlight was filtered to a soft blue at their depth.

After, they had a cold *Tecate* and walked along the quay.

"Tiki was just so helpful," she gushed. "Did you see the Hawks Bill turtle he pointed out?"

Joel shrugged. "Tiki didn't really pay that much attention to the rest of us."

She felt the little sting. "Mm. Sorry. You're right. My first time. I'll get better." Her eyes were as blue as his, her dark blond hair sun-bleached like his.

"I'm leaving for Merida tomorrow," he said.

"Ooh! I want to go to Chichen-Itza! Can I go with you?"

It wasn't what he'd been thinking, but he was alone, and having her along might be fun. "OK. But the ferry to Playa del Carmen leaves right at 7 a.m." Like she might have trouble getting there on time.

He walked her back to the place where she was staying and slid his arm around her waist. She turned her face to him, a trace of skepticism in her look. She was tall, almost as tall as he was. On the sidewalk, just outside the halo of a streetlight, a tarantula the size of a dinner plate rested on the warm cement.

The next morning, she felt light-headed and feverish. There was a bus after the ferry. It was crowded and hot, and baskets of live chickens were crammed overhead. At the jungle stops, groups of Maya climbed aboard with more baggage.

Seven hours later, in Merida, she was so ill that she had to depend entirely on him to find them a hotel. He brought her some *asperina* from a neighborhood *farmacia*.

It took another two days for her to really feel better. He brought her food and water and explored the city by himself.

More out of gratitude at the very beginning, she embraced him in the bed they had been sharing and began to show him what she liked. He was a quick study, and she, after the days of sweats and fever and sickness, was not anticipating the intensity of her body's response to him. She wanted him, and had him, again and again.

They climbed the steps of the great pyramid at Chichen-Itza, and in the evening, ate tapas at a sidewalk restaurant in Merida. The transom over the tall door of their hotel room was open, and her cries in bed with him at night carried out into the corridor and down in to the lobby, or so it appeared from the barely concealed smiles of the desk clerk and bellhops.

"You're going to kill me, woman," he groaned as she pulled him to her again.

A week or so later, back in Cozumel, they embraced for the last time. His taxi was waiting to take him the short distance to the airport. He had joined the Army and was scheduled to report when he returned home to Florida. He did not suggest exchanging contact information, so after an instant of hesitation, she decided not to ask for his. As his taxi pulled away, she walked over to the boat for her last day of diving at the reef.

That evening, she strolled alone on the quay as the sky turned purple and the clouds piled up over the sea. She went back to the hotel on Calle 3 Sur. I'll never see him again, she thought as she lay on the bed they had shared that morning. His scent was still in the sheets.

Chapter 1
About 25 Years Ago in Florida

He was a tall kid with thick glasses. He belonged to the chess club and the computer club, according to the high school yearbook. He enjoyed building FM radios. He wore crew neck sweaters over a shirt and tie almost every day, but he was too big to really bully. Sometimes other kids tried to needle him with nerd jokes, but he mainly took these as their unwitting compliments. He knew how smart he was, and he knew how dumb his would-be tormentors were, so he wasn't really bothered.

His father had been another matter.

He was born up in Pittsburgh. His parents were older by then, quite a bit older than most other kids' parents. His father was big brute of a man who had apparently managed to conceal his vile nature from his wife until after they were married, and she was pregnant.

He could never remember a time at home when he wasn't frightened or angry or overwhelmed until he made a small discovery about himself when he was eight. He felt better, sometimes even good, when he stomped on some little creature whose misfortune it was to have attracted his notice. Bugs. Worms. A baby bird that had fallen from its nest while its parents screamed. There was nothing they could do.

    A soft, white cloud seemed to settle down and softened the pain during a particularly brutal beating that took place while his mother fluttered helplessly in the kitchen. His thoughts started to flow as if in a stream of light. He wasn't in his body anymore. He could see what the days would be like if his father just wasn't in the family anymore.

    He was still on the floor and his mother was applying a cool, damp dish cloth to his head.

    "Mummy," he said, "did you know that seventy-eight percent of all murders are committed by a member of the family or by somebody the guy knows?"

    "I don't think your father would kill you," she whispered.

    He was thirteen or fourteen when his occasional memory lapses seemed to maybe become evident to other people. Every so often, he would find himself in his room wearing different clothes than he had put on. Or his mother would insist that she had told him about something she wanted him to do, and she was really disappointed that he had forgotten, because he had promised. He would apologize, but, in truth, he had no recollection. Or he would kind of "come to" without having any actual memory of leaving Spanish class, yet here he was in Mr. Cody's algebra class. He learned to deflect others' questions or to laugh them off.

"I guess I'm just a space cadet," he would joke at school. Privately, he worried that the beatings might be harming his ability to think clearly.

"I need to start making some changes right away," he said aloud to himself in his bedroom, as he soldered wires into place in the ham radio he was building. "First of all, I'll have to devise my plan. And next, I'll need to do a practice run. Maybe even two."

A month later, he sat with his mother at the Presbyterian church for Mr. Schenck's funeral. Mr. Schenck had been old, over eighty, and had lived alone in a house in their neighborhood for at least thirty years. He had been pretty mean to some of the neighborhood kids who made too much noise. One day, the boy who cut his lawn every Tuesday had found his back door open.

It would have been too bad, awful really, if, in the heat of the Florida summer, the body hadn't been found right away.

It appeared that Mr. Schenck had hit his head on the edge of his kitchen countertop. The medical examiner, people said, thought he had died shortly after falling. It was a shame, the neighbors agreed, because Mr. Schenck had kept to himself and was quiet.

His own father died suddenly, several months later, in the garage. Apparently, he had fallen and hit his head on the concrete. He didn't come in for dinner, and he didn't come in to watch the news.

At nine o'clock, his mother put on her night gown and removed her dentures. "Tell your father when he comes in if you're still up that I've gone to bed."

"OK, Mummy. Sleep well."

A little while later, he took a thorough shower and started on his geometry homework. There really was no point, he thought, in saying anything to his father.

Chapter 2
I'm Still in a Fog

Catherine Cameron met Charlie Crane at the first meeting she ever attended of the North Tampa Bromeliad Society. His name badge said he was the membership chairman. He invited her to sign up for the Society's monthly newsletter and offered her a cup of brewed coffee.

"I take it black, thanks." She wrote her name and email address on the clipboard he handed her. He looked at it.

"Address?"

"I'd rather be contacted by telephone or email. I live in Seminole Heights."

He was strikingly handsome with a good haircut. He dressed with a casual flair and liked exotic plants. Catherine smiled warmly at him. She assumed he was gay.

He followed her over to the refreshments table.

"What kinds of bromeliads do you like? Lately, I've been growing orthophytums and some Hectias. In pots, mainly."

"Do you live nearby?" she asked.

"Not that near. I live up in Pasco, in Dade City. I volunteer at the botanical gardens at the university, so I'm down here quite a bit."

Catherine noticed the gold ring on his finger. "Does your partner enjoy plants, too?"

"My partner?" Charlie stared at her. "I live with my mother, but I'm not gay."

"OK." She made a little gesture with her shoulder. "What do you do for work?"

"I'm not really working right now, except for some substitute teaching. So, I have plenty of time for my plants. You?"

"I work. At the university. I also really like the botanical gardens there."

Catherine started to walk away, dismissing him with a slight smile. She studied the bromeliads members had brought in for the display tables.

Charlie followed. "Do *you* have a partner? A husband?"

"I had a husband. He died."

"I'm sorry."

"Me, too."

"I don't want to upset you. I'm sorry I said anything."

"No need. I probably won't even remember this conversation. I'm still sort of in a fog."

He had a nice way about him. "I think I understand. My mom lost her husband. I didn't want her to be all alone in that big place, so I live with her. She's doing pretty well for being over eighty."

"She's lucky she has you. I'm finding it really takes a lot to keep up a house. The yardwork. The maintenance. I hope I'll be able to manage it."

Charlie nodded. "It is a lot. Well, I have to stop at the pharmacy for my mom's prescription, so I need to get going. Good luck with your plants."

They walked outside together. "See you," she said. She pulled out of the dark parking lot in what looked like a red classic Mustang convertible.

Charlie inhaled a soft whistle and watched her drive off. One of her taillights was a little dim.

Chapter 3

I Like It Here

Joel Miller had been hired by the Hialeah Police Department while he was still in the Reserves.

He had a knack for languages and had been trained at the Defense Language Institute in California to a level of functional proficiency in Russian and German. Back in Florida, however, there was little call for anything but Spanish. This was in the time before Russians with shady money had infiltrated the South Florida luxury real estate market.

Fairly soon, he started to feel some of the weight of being a cop in the city where he'd grown up. One of the toughest parts of the job was the impact it had had on his friendships. It wasn't so much that his old friends no longer trusted him with their secrets and their petty crimes. He had expected this and remembered with a degree of amusement how they'd all acted around the cops in the neighborhood back when he was a kid with them. What he hadn't really been prepared for was how being a cop would gradually change the way he viewed other people, the citizenry in general, as well as other cops and certainly some of his old friends.

But initially he'd felt mainly pride in having a job that allowed him to be able to protect and serve in his own community. He was named Officer of the Month not long after he joined the force for his role in capturing two men who had been involved in a stabbing incident over near the old Hialeah racetrack.

As Joel advanced in his law enforcement career, his supervisor suggested that he think about making a transfer to Internal Affairs. Joel was not naive. He knew the main players, and he understood departmental politics. He doubted that his superiors' enthusiasm for cleaning up any corruption among the rank and file would extend very far up the chain of command. Nevertheless, he took the job, expecting at some point that he would pay dearly.

The first casualty of this career move was his relationship with his younger brother. Emil had been a very good-looking kid. He had golden curls and a dazzling white smile. He had their mother's cute nose, rather than the more aquiline one Joel had inherited from their father. Emil was his mother's baby boy, and although she saw through Emil's lazy promises and his inconsistent relationship with facts, she had rarely supported Joel back when they were kids. Joel eventually stopped bringing her evidence of Emil's untrustworthiness.

After a halfhearted four semesters at Dade County Junior College, which resulted in a degree primarily because so many of his instructors passed him through, Emil decided that he, too, wanted to join the city police force. He used Joel's good reputation as a reference of sorts. Emil, however, was a lazy cop. He didn't like the paperwork--their mother had claimed without evidence that he was dyslexic—and he didn't like patrolling the neighborhoods in the hot sun. He did, however, like working vice. Joel distanced himself—it was a large department by then--fully expecting the worst at some point.

Several years after joining the force, when he certainly understood the potential consequences, Emil approved a request outside of official channels to return a 9mm Beretta to its owner. Joel had personally ordered that gun held, pending investigation. The gun's owner was an old friend of Emil's from high school. It was near the end of a long shift, and the young property clerk on duty that day was inexperienced, and, most likely, was persuaded by Emil's flirtatious attention to her.

That property clerk, or some unknown person, had included—whether accidentally or otherwise was not conclusively determined--a copy of a list of departmental officers' home telephone numbers along with the disgruntled Beretta owner's paperwork. That confidential list was subsequently distributed on the street as a form of misplaced revenge by the gun owner. Joel, who had written the original report, was technically responsible for its chain of custody as well as for that of the Beretta. He was officially reprimanded. Emil did not ever own up to his role in the mix-up, if that's what it actually was, and Joel only raised the issue with him once.

Joel's feelings about the incident did not fully dissipate; he remained angry and disgusted, both with his brother and with the department. After talking it over with a friend on the force, he decided after a few months to resign and take a new position outside the immediate area with the Monroe County Sheriff's Department.

When Joel told his wife, Carmella, what he had decided, she was silent.

She had a small career in real estate sales, and she loved their house in Kendall. Her family, Bolivian immigrants, lived close by, and weekly family gatherings were a way of life in their community. He had not consulted her about the job change.

"How far is it?"

Joel shrugged. "About an hour or two or maybe three, depending. Three twelve-hour shifts. It's Tavernier, for the most part. There will be quite a bit of driving on the job. That county's more than a hundred miles long."

Carmella considered for a moment. "OK. We can stay here, and you can commute."

"I would have to get an address somewhere in Monroe. I wouldn't have to be there all the time, just mainly on my duty days."

Carmella was quiet for several minutes while Joel scrolled through his messages. Finally, she said, "This is about your brother, right?"

"That's some of it."

"And the rest of it? You're still angry at the department? Is it about us?"

"It's not about us. You might like the Keys."

"We'll see. I like it here."

Chapter 4
Sometimes They Leave Presents

Catherine had just come in from outside when Charlie called. She'd been cleaning up the side yard. There was a pile of plastic pots and some left-over debris from the very last project her late husband had finished--repairing the safety bars on the bedroom windows. In Tampa, it was cool enough some of the year to leave windows open at night, but the Seminole Heights neighborhood didn't always feel secure enough to Catherine, especially now that she was alone.

An oak tree's spreading canopy kept the front of the house dark at night, filtering light from the nearest streetlamp. Her house was by an out-of-the-way city park where kids and who-knows-who-else hung out at night by the cool Hillsborough River.

"Hi. It's me."

"I'm sorry. Who is this?'

"Charlie. We met the other night...."

Catherine was silent.

"At the Bromeliad Society...."

"Oh, oh, oh. Sorry. I didn't recognize your voice."

"I thought I'd call to see how your new plants are doing."

"Actually, I was just going through some pots I have out back, sort of making an inventory for planting them. I have a nice, screened porch. It already has a lot of ferns."

"Sounds like you have shade."

"I do, up close to the house. Farther out, I have a grapefruit tree. My husband loved grapefruit. He made grapefruit juice. We had...I have...a citrus juicer."

"Would you like some help with anything?"

"I don't know. There's an old wood pile in the back that I need to get cleaned up, but I don't have a good way to get the wood out of here. The trash guy won't take it."

"Hey, I have a pickup truck available. When do you want me to come over?"

"Oh, you don't need to bother. I'll figure something out. Maybe I could convince the City..."

"I'd like to."

She hesitated. "I guess on the weekend, if it wouldn't be asking too much."

"Okay. How about Friday evening? That way I could take the wood for recycling on Saturday. They make mulch out of it."

"Alright. Thanks. I live at..."

"I know. I looked it up."

Charlie arrived Friday a little after seven. He was dressed in jeans and a dark maroon dress shirt. They loaded the wood into his truck. It took almost an hour. He sweated through his shirt.

"How about if I order us a pizza?" Catherine suggested.

Charlie stepped closer and bent his head to kiss her. Catherine froze and then decided to kiss him back. Briefly. Rocky, Catherine's Siamese cat, watched from the kitchen island.

"I like cats," Charlie commented, scratching Rocky's ears. "If they like you back, they sometimes leave you presents."

Catherine cocked her head and shrugged.

"You know. Like the mice they catch. Showing you that they're doing their job, ridding the area of vermin."

"Well, Rocky never goes out, so I don't get those kinds of little gifts."

Charlie smiled. "I have to go, but I'll see you tomorrow after I drop off the wood? We could have that pizza then."

The next afternoon, Catherine made a point of showering but put on jeans and a casual tee shirt. Charlie arrived at 5:30 with a six-pack of premium beer. Catherine ordered the pizza from a place on Florida Avenue.

After they ate, Charlie said, "Once again, I have to go. But I noticed your soffits could use some repair in places and also some paint." She walked him out to the driveway, and he pointed to an area over the kitchen window.

"See? You're getting some rot, or at least softening of the wood."

"Hmm. I didn't know."

"It's always something with houses."

***

Joel rented a small cottage on the bay side of Plantation Key. He brought Carmella down to take a look.

"It's okay for a single guy."

"I'm not a single guy. We live in Kendall. This is just for when I have to be here a few days a week for the job. It won't be forever."

She put her arms around him, and he kissed the top of her head. Her hair smelled like camellias.

Chapter 5
A Boy Scout

Charlie prepped and painted Catherine's soffits the next weekend. She had called around for estimates and handed him a check.

"What's this for?"

"For your work."

"No, no, no. I enjoyed it. I like to keep busy."

"I really want you to take it. You deserve to be paid for your work."

"Nope. How about if you just cook me dinner?"

"Well. I'm not actually much of a cook. We could go out..."

"Or order another pizza..."

After they ate on the porch, the house was dark. They hadn't turned on any lights. Charlie started toward the front door, and then turned to Catherine.

"I really like you."

He pulled her close, surprising her, and kissed her.

After a while, he led her to the bedroom. They kept their clothes on. They continued kissing, but Catherine was feeling unsettled, not passionate. When it was time to go farther, she stopped.

"I can't."

He was breathing heavily. "OK."

He looked darkly handsome under the porch light as she sent him home.

"Drive safe."

Catherine went about her activities. That evening and the next day, thoughts about Charlie kept intruding. She finally sat down to try to figure out how she felt. Why wasn't she stirred by this good-looking, helpful, intelligent man? She apparently wasn't ready for a new relationship. But, more than that, she had felt no desire for him at all. His kisses were warm. He was very handsome with his dark hair and his striking light blue eyes. He was smart, an amusing conversationalist, and nice and helpful and polite. A total Boy Scout. But that bit of mysterious something that ignites when the chemistry is right was not there.

When he called again, Catherine told him what she thought. As kindly as she could, she explained that she didn't see a future for them as romantic partners. Charlie, thankfully, said he understood, and seemed to take it lightly.

Two evenings later, he turned up on her porch with Cuban take-out and a bottle of red wine.

Catherine hesitated, and then didn't let him in. "We can't do this tonight. I don't want you to think that I don't like you. I'm just not ready for anything like this."

Charlie looked sad standing there, holding the wine and food that he'd brought.

"I'm sorry. I hope you can understand." He'd driven thirty-five miles to see her. She sighed and let him in, and they ate the pulled pork with yellow rice and black beans and drank a glass of *Castillo del Wayjay*. Catherine's Siamese cat, Rocky, hung around the table looking for a handout.

After, Catherine said, "You're a nice guy. We can be friends. But, please, please, please, don't just drop over here anymore unannounced."

The next evening, Catherine tensed when the doorbell rang. It was Charlie again.

"Hi! I was just in the neighborhood……"

"Charlie, we cannot do this. *I* can't do this. It has to stop."

"I don't understand."

"I told you. When you were here last night. I'm not ready for a relationship…with you, or with anyone else at all. I'm just not. So… I'm sorry, but no."

She shut the door. After a while, he left.

Two nights later, he called and invited her to see a movie.

"There's a screening of that Ingrid Bergman movie you said you liked at the theater near you on Sligh Avenue."

"No, thank you," Catherine said.

"Can you just explain to me why?"

"I already have. I'm not interested in a relationship right now."

On Saturday night, he showed up again. Catherine took a harder tone with him, hoping to finally push him away. "Please don't come over. You can't just show up like this," she said, and shut the door as he stood on her porch looking devastated. Eventually, he drove away.

A half an hour later, she glanced out the kitchen window over the sink as she was cleaning Rocky's cat dishes. It was dark, but she could see him from the illumination of a nearby streetlight, pacing back and forth, back and forth, in front of her house.

"This is nuts." Catherine called the Tampa Police Department and told the dispatcher that there was a man outside her house bothering her.

The patrol car showed up fairly quickly. She said that she was a widow and was alone in the house. That she knew Charlie casually, but now he was calling and coming over uninvited and she was getting concerned about her safety and his mental health.

The cops spoke with Charlie for a while. She could see through the window that he was crying and agitated.

One of the officers came back up to her door.

"He says he just wants to talk to you. He says he wants to know 'why'."

Catherine shook her head. "No more explanations. I've told him why." She appealed to the officer. "He's weird. I don't know him that well. My husband died of cancer. I'm here alone. I don't want to see him, and I don't want to talk to him."

Rocky rubbed against her leg, and she picked the cat up. Charlie was still on the street talking animatedly with the other cop.

The officer at the door looked doubtfully back at Charlie. "He's allowed to walk on the street. It's a public road."

"He doesn't live anywhere near here," Catherine said firmly. "He lives in Dade City. He came all the way down to Tampa, forty miles, just to walk up and down in front of my house. Doesn't that seem kind of nuts to you? I don't want to end up dead like in one of those movies where the cops say they can't do anything."

After about ten more minutes, Charlie and the police drove off in their own vehicles. She kept the outdoor lights on all night.

Catherine heard nothing more from Charlie, although she suspected that two hang-up calls could have been from him. On Thursday, when she got home from work, she found a dead squirrel. It had been carefully placed on her doormat. A black ribbon had been tied around its neck. She called the police.

"Unless you have a surveillance camera, you can't really prove it was him."

"Why should I have to spend money to prove this guy is harassing me?"

"It might be worth it if it happens again. Otherwise, there is nothing to tie your boyfriend to this."

"Not. My. Boyfriend."

Rocky rubbed against her leg. The officer looked down at the cat.

"Does the cat go out?"

"No, he stays inside. He only goes out on the screened porch. I have some ferns out there that he likes to lie in….do you think…?"

The officer shrugged. "No telling."

Catherine considered moving away from the area. She was finding it sad, actually, living in the house that she had shared with her husband. They had bought it after he had gotten sick, because it was close to his cancer treatment resources and close to where she worked at the University. She really didn't have any roots yet in the neighborhood. Her job was just OK. She had dreamed for more than twenty years of someday living in the Florida Keys. She called her friend from work.

"You should go," Tanya said. "Working here kind of sucks, in comparison with living in the Keys. You could rent out your house in case you ever want to come back to Tampa. Rent some place down there. Try it out. Give it a shot. I could come visit. We could hit the bars, have some fun in the sun."

"Ha. I'll probably be *working* in a bar.... real jobs are hard to come by down there."

Catherine found a two-bedroom duplex on an open-water channel in Marathon and had no problem getting hired for a server job at the Sparkling Tarpon, not too far away.

Two weeks later, she and Rocky were living in the Florida Keys. The job didn't pay very well, but the tips were good once she started to get to know the regulars, and she could eat and drink on the house after her shift. The duplex was expensive, but the clear, warm, aqua water was everywhere, and the intense sun was burning away some of her sadness.

"Trade-offs," Rick, the bartender, told her.

One of the regulars nodded sagely. "I traded my wife and my house up in Opa-locka for a fishing boat down here."

Chapter 6
She Probably Already Made Bail

At 10:59 on a Thursday night, Joel had a Ferrari F8 *Tributo* pulled over just south of Mile Marker 80 on the Overseas Highway. He had clocked it at 85 mph. The driver passed the field sobriety tests and had the *cojones* to ask Joel for some Key West nightlife recommendations.

Joel kept an eye on the passenger, another Cuban guy in his thirties. "I don't go down there much." He returned the license and registration and wrote out a ticket for a costly forty miles an hour over the speed limit.

"Fucking asshole," the driver muttered as he pulled out into the humid night.

A little later, while Joel was still in Islamorada headed south, a call came in for Sector 6 support at the Tarpon Creek Poolside Inn. Joel took off, lights flashing, siren off. "What is it?"

"Signal 7".

The victim was a white female, possibly in her sixties, although it was difficult to assess. She had head and facial injuries.

"He must not have liked her much," remarked a first responder at the scene.

"Looks it."

They had finished handing it over to the investigative team when a 10-66 came in.

The address was in Marathon.

"Complaint from female. Reports a Caucasian male seen parked across the street. Dead bird on the porch."

"I really don't have time for this tonight," Joel told the dispatcher.

***

Marco scrolled through the latest Monroe County, Florida arrests on the Sheriff's Department public website. He yawned and slapped his bare leg. "Fucking bugs. Why are we sitting out here in the dark?"

"Language, asshole. My kid's here." The other man, hair starting to gray and maybe thirty pounds overweight, lazily gestured to a skinny kid playing games on a cell phone.

"So, listen to this," Marco continued.

"Alonzo Basulto. 25. Black male. Groundskeeper. Arrested Fleming Street, Key West. 1 felony count of

784.021a-Aggravated Assault—with deadly weapon without intent to kill."

"Harry Conley, 39. Address: Streets of Key West. Occupation: Construction. Arrested 500 Duval Street, Key West. One misdemeanor count of 843.02 Resisting Officer Obstruct w/o Violence."

"So? Fucking morons."

"I'm not done.

"Kelly Ann Morrison, 29. Address: Marathon, FL. Occupation: Home security. Arrest location: Trinidad Street, Key West. Misdemeanor count of 784.03.1a1 Battery."

"So?"

"So, look at the mugshot."

"Chick looks high. So what?"

"Who's she look like?" Marco pressed.

"I don't know. Some hooker?"

"It says she's in security. Why do you have to denigrate everyone? Look closer."

"It's that chick who was at the Blue Oyster the other night." Olivera paused, gazing into the back of the overgrown yard. "So what?"

"So, what if she saw something? What if she decides to, like, cooperate?"

"All she's got is a bullshit misdemeanor charge. She has zero reason to 'cooperate.' Nor, for that matter, would they have any reason to make her an offer."

"She might've seen something."

"Like what? Oh, like you totally unnecessarily shanking that poor old shrimper behind the trash dumpster? Because you were drunk and stupid and have no impulse control?" Olivera shook his head. "And now—days later-- you're still all loco over some girl maybe saw it, and what? Is just keeping it to herself? Don't you fucking think she'd have already said something if she'd seen it, if she was going to? What do you want me to do? Bail her out so you can one-eighty-seven her?"

"She probably already made bail."

Olivera shrugged. "Do what you want. Just try not to do anything too moronic or get me involved. I'm not going back to jail. I've got my kid here to take care of."

***

Kelly Anne Morrison, Kate since seventh grade, was the granddaughter of a popular former governor of Florida. She had legally changed her last name the day after she graduated from the University of Central Florida with a degree in computer science and moved from the family home near Tallahassee down to the Florida Keys.

Her mother had reacted with philosophical disappointment. The family consensus was that she would "find herself" and "settle down."

Kate had tended bar at some of the joints in Old Town for a while before she'd recently decided to leave the drunk-tourist craziness of Key West and moved up to Marathon. She was studying for her Six Pack Captain's License and was working at a small cybersecurity start-up. Wealthy seasonal residents in the Middle Keys wanted their winter homes to have the latest and best security. Currently, she was evaluating a new thermal imaging system at her rented duplex. And some inventions of her own that no one needed to know about yet.

When Catherine got home from her shift at the Sparkling Tarpon that evening, there was a sheriff's cruiser in the driveway next door, and her neighbor, Kate, was talking to the deputy.

Catherine went inside her unit and turned on the lights. A few minutes later, there was a knock on her door. Kate invited herself in.

"Do you have anything to drink?"

Catherine pulled a bottle of grocery store white wine from the refrigerator.

"You'll never believe this," Kate said, taking a swallow. "I get home from work and there's a dead seagull on my porch. With a pink string tied on it. I really don't need any weird shit like that right now. I've got a court case, and a technical issue with my new imaging system's signal processing…. speaking of which…want to take a peek at what we might have picked up? I probably should have showed the cops, but I didn't want them to know I have it."

Kate looked at Catherine directly for the first time. "What's the matter with you? You look...funny."

"The seagull. What about the seagull?"

"It was dead. You a bird-lover?"

"Not overly. You said a string. What did it look like?"

"More like a pink ribbon. And there was a guy in a car parked across the street, angled so he could pull away fast. Which he did."

"What did the guy look like?"

Kate shrugged. "No idea. It was dark. All of this I told the cop."

"What are they going to do?"

"Nothing, most likely." She stood up to go. "You OK?"

"You have...an imaging system?"

"Oh, yeah. It's thermal imaging, heat, you know? It picks up heat, and shape to some degree. It's how they found the Boston Marathon bomber hiding in a boat."

"You can tell who it is?"

"No, no... they knew who they were looking for...otherwise, just the shape of a body or a fox or whatever. Come on over to my place, and we'll have a look."

Kate fiddled with her laptop for a bit. "Here he is."

A ghostly white shimmering shape appeared on the walkway, knelt, and placed something dark on Kate's step.

"That's all?"

"'All'? These things are actually awesome. You can find termite infestations, lost pets, underfloor heating, overheating motors, the list goes on. Who is he, anyway?"

Catherine hesitated. "I don't really know...."

"Come on. You must have some idea.... you should have seen the look on your face when I said, 'dead seagull.' Or, I guess, it was more when I mentioned the string."

"There was a guy bothering me up in Tampa."

"No way! That creepy guy you told me about? Came all the way down here? Let's get the cops back, pronto...but...I am leaving you my laptop to show them if necessary and...I'm getting out of here. I had a little dust-up down in Key West a while back, and I do not need to be involved in this, if it entails cops. Which it will. Call them! Now! Bye! Do not let them take my computer. Or copy anything from it. Say it's yours. I was not here, OK? The dead bird's off near the hibiscus where I tossed it."

Chapter 7
What Is Your Emergency?

Kate took off, and Catherine called 911.

"Monroe County. What is your emergency?"

"Not sure if it is an emergency, but there was a Deputy here a few minutes ago, and I forgot to give him some information..."

"Address?"

Catherine told the dispatcher and waited anxiously. What could she possibly report that wouldn't make her sound hysterical? A guy she knew followed her from Tampa and was stalking her? What proof did she have? The thermal image was definitely something, and it was the same kind of dead-animal-by-the-front-door incident as had happened up in Tampa. But Kate was afraid for some reason that they'd confiscate her equipment if Catherine showed it to them.

A Monroe County Sheriff's white vehicle pulled up, and Catherine nervously stepped outside. The night was humid, with a slight breeze that fluttered the leaves of the banana tree just outside her front door. Moonlight shifted through the coconut palm fronds rustling overhead.

The deputy was sitting in his car, on the radio. After a few minutes, he got out of the vehicle and walked up to the doorstep to begin his inquiry. Catherine suddenly felt foolish.

"Sorry to call you back again...you spoke to my neighbor, Kate. I think a guy has been stalking me from Tampa," she continued, "and leaving dead animals. I realize that sounds weird, and I don't know if it's even a crime, but.... that's why the call back. My neighbor saw someone that could have been him in a car a little while ago."

"Name, please, ma'am." The deputy looked at the duplex, re-checking the address.

"Oh, um, Charlie. His last name is Crane."

"*Your* name, ma'am."

"Catherine Cameron. I just moved here from Tampa. This whole thing is...well.... my husband died a while ago, and this guy Charlie...well, it's kind of complicated. But he started stalking me and leaving dead animals. I think. And now it's happening again. I'm sorry, me just saying it out loud makes me hear myself sounding crazy."

"Can you please point out the animal again?"

"This one's a bird. It has a ribbon around its neck, like the squirrel did up in Tampa. It was left on my neighbor's porch. This is a duplex. Side A and Side B."

Catherine extended her hand. "It's still there, in the bushes, where my neighbor tossed it."

"Did you file a report up in Tampa?"

"Yes...I guess there was a report. A Tampa officer came over, and he talked to him. The guy. Charlie. That was before the dead squirrel. I'm not sure about a report. I did call, more than once."

The deputy made notes, put on plastic gloves, and knelt down. He took photos of the seagull with a small digital camera and stood back up.

"What happens now?" asked Catherine.

"I write a report." He handed Catherine his business card. "Call if there's anything else."

Catherine turned to look at the card under the porch light and read aloud, "Joel...Miller."

Something about the way she said his name caused him to turn back, and the way the porch light caught her face sent his heart rate speeding.

"I...I'm Catherine. Are you...Joel...from Mexico?"

She was still slender, but her blond hair was lighter than he remembered and was cut shorter. The twenty or so years had given her more voluptuous curves and added just a few lines around her mouth and eyes. She was holding his gaze, and he could see her assessing what the time had done to him. A line

48

from *Raiders of the Lost Ark* popped into his head: '*It's not the years, it's the mileage.*'

Catherine said, "...Joel...do you...live here?"

"South of Miami. But I'm working in Monroe County, now."

His eyes took her in, and she could feel her face flushing. She wished she had put on nicer clothes and had done a little more with her makeup and her hair...or something.

He had shorter hair, too. His body had filled out. His shoulders and chest were broader and well-muscled, but his waist and hips were still trim. He wore the khaki uniform shirt and the gold badge of the county sheriff's department, and a holstered Glock 9mm.

The radio in his patrol car crackled something Catherine couldn't really hear.

"I need to go. I'll check back with you." He pulled away with the cruiser's red and blue lights flashing. Catherine watched him leave, feeling agitated, light-headed, and very much incomplete.

Down the street, a slow-moving vehicle wheeled over and parked.

Joel pulled out onto US 1 and headed toward the Lobster Hut Motel and Bar up the Overseas Highway. He left on his blue and red flashers but drove at a prudent speed on the dangerous road. No point in risking the life of anyone else. This victim was already dead.

A half a block away from Catherine's duplex, a vehicle remained parked under the deep shadows of a forty-foot-tall black olive tree. The driver settled in to await developments. He lowered the passenger window a bit to get a clearer look at the duplex.

When Joel arrived at the Lobster Hut, his friend Paz was already at the scene.

"What do we have?"

Paz shrugged. "Seventy-two-year-old white female. Deceased. Severe head injury. Probable weapon tire iron or something similar. Not found at the scene. Victim discovered by a customer going to her own vehicle."

"Robbery?"

Paz shrugged again. "No cash in the wallet, but ID and credit cards intact."

"Witnesses?"

"She-Meredith Anthony-was seen drinking at the Tiki bar. Not a regular. Registration matches the SUV she was found near. Polk County. Checked in to the motel two nights ago. Due to check out tomorrow."

"Traveling with anyone else?"

"She was seen drinking with a younger man, tall, dark hair, according to the pm wait staff. Unknown if the UNSUB was checked in to the motel as well."

"Security cameras?" Joel and Paz looked around, and seeing none, went inside to interview the desk clerk.

"Nope. We could use a camera outback -- every so often there is a vehicle break-in—but you'd have to talk to the boss about why we don't have one."

Joel turned to Paz. "Did she have jewelry?"

"She was found wearing a gold chain, gold earrings, and a ring with a blue stone."

Joel hesitated and then asked, "Any type of a dead animal nearby?"

"Nope, nothing like that. What are you getting at?" Paz asked. "A little dog or something?"

"No, no. It's just...unusual," Joel said. "There are so few murders or suspicious deaths in this county. Or so I was told when I took the job. Motor vehicles, boats, bicycles, pedestrian fatalities…. lots. Plus, drownings, and some overdoses are basically what we get down here in 'paradise,' correct?"

Paz nodded. "Right. We have deaths from cancer here, heart disease, like any place else, motor vehicle accidents….and suicide. Highest rate of both motor vehicle accidents and suicide in the state. Alcohol tends to be the common denominator. Murder...not so much."

"Who usually does the investigations?"

"We do," Paz replied, "unless it is suspicious enough, or uncertain enough, and then we bring in the Florida Department of Law Enforcement. Which almost never happens since the suspicious death rate here is virtually nil."

"What would we do with this case?" Joel asked.

"Let it ride up the chain of command and see where it stops. Maybe the FDLE will come in. We don't have a reasonable suspect at this point."

"What about the guy she was seen drinking with?"

Paz shrugged. "This is a bar in the Keys. People come, and people go. Wait staff notices how they tip, is about all. We could ask."

"She tipped OK," Sue, the waitress, recalled. "Used a credit card. Drank vodka tonics."

"Was there anyone with her? Talk to anyone?"

"She talked with everyone. This is a Tiki bar in the Keys. You drink and you bullshit."

"Anyone in particular?"

"Nope."

Joel realized then that he had failed to get a description of the Tampa stalker from Catherine.

Catherine. He would need to go back again to interview her about what had happened in Tampa. He felt his lips start to swell at the thought of seeing her again.

Chapter 8
Emil and Carmella

Carmella sat out by the pool as the evening began to settle in. Coco, her little Bichon, lay nearby on the still-warm concrete pool deck. The underwater lights were on, and as the surface of the pool water rippled and shifted, the light cast waves of bluish green around the back yard. The palm trees were up-lit. Soft Latin music wafted in from a nearby yard in the neighborhood.

Carmella sipped her strong vodka and tonic and scrolled through her messages. One canceled house-showing tomorrow. Someone wanted to see a condo she had listed at 2:30 instead of three. Joel had texted earlier, saying he wouldn't be back until Friday, most likely.

At 8 pm, Emil texted to say he would be coming by to chat in a while.

Emil. Carmella had known Joel's little brother since they were in high school together. She had sat next to him in ninth grade, in Mr. Ortega's earth science class…. rocks, glaciers, global warming, volcanoes. She, and probably every other girl in the class, had had a terrible crush on him.

Emil had the whitest smile, tooth paste commercial white, and the sexiest lips. Girls would tell jokes and flirt and do whatever they could to try to get him to turn that smile their way. He was the first boy Carmella had ever wanted to go out with, but she was just one of a long string for him.

Emil had gotten Kelly Perez pregnant when she was fifteen and he was sixteen. Her Cuban grandfather might have actually killed Emil, but Kelly enlisted her uncles' and her grandmother's support. She had the baby, and her Tia Esme adopted the little girl. They named her Rosa Maria. The family moved up the coast to Coral Terrace.

After Kelly, Emil was much more consistent about using condoms, but he was just as careless with girls' hearts. It wasn't so much that he was mean or unkind. He had a seemingly bottomless need for the kind of affirmation that he got from females buzzing around him, and, in all fairness, his seductive scent, or whatever it was that kept the women coming around, was perhaps not really all his fault.

Two years after high school, Carmella began dating Emil's older brother, Joel. Joel was in the Reserves back then, in a special operations unit, and was away at least one weekend a month and two weeks in the summer for readiness training. He was twenty-four years old, and she was twenty.

Joel was serious about Carmella. They went to the beach together and lay on brightly colored towels on the hot sand. Carmella carefully applied sunscreen to Joel's fair skin, and they talked about a future together. Joel gave her a necklace with two gold hearts intertwined.

In July, about six months after they had moved in together, Joel's reserve unit was sent to Iraq. It was initially scheduled to be a short deployment. Joel asked Carmella if she would wait for him, and she said she would. She was keeping the books for her family's car repair business and studying for her real estate sales license.

Weeks passed with only irregular contact from Joel. His mission took him to remote locations with poor communications infrastructure. Carmella had never done well on her own. She became sad and achingly needy. Her mother, possibly from some experience of her own in the past that she had never talked about, told Carmella that soldiers, sailors, and marines had a girl in every port.

One Friday evening, Emil came by Carmella and Joel's apartment with a bottle of white rum. Emil was still in junior college then, but he wasn't making a lot of progress toward getting enough credits to graduate.

He sat next to her on the brown leather couch and mixed her a rum and coke on the coffee table with lots of ice and a wedge of lime. There was soft Miami music on the radio, and the lights were low.

They drank and talked for a while about the people they'd known in high school - where they were and what they were doing. Emil confessed that he regretted not having had the chance to get to know her better back then.

Carmella laughed. "You had every chance. Every day, you had a chance. All you would have had to do back then was ask. Nicely."

Emil took her hand. "Carmelita. I was a stupid kid. I'm sorry if I ever hurt you."

"You didn't hurt me. You missed out."

Emil put his index finger under her chin, and said, "You look so pretty in your rose-colored blouse." He lazily drew his finger down along the side of her throat, and, keeping eye contact with her, pulled aside the low neckline, exposing her nipple under her sheer bra. He raised his eyebrows and gave her one of his rakish smiles.

"I know I missed out. I was such a foolish boy." He gently plucked the lacy fabric of her bra aside, and took her nipple with his lips, sucking and tugging, and pulling her to him, until she was squirming with desire for him.

"We can't do this, Emil. I don't want to."

Emil gently released her after a final kiss with his full lips and pulled the top of her lacy bra back up. He slid his hand under her skirt, up her thigh, and expertly slipped a finger under her panties. He withdrew his finger, now slippery wet, and said softly, "No, you really don't want to do this with me, do you, *Chica*?"

After that, Emil would drop by sometimes, but intermittently and always at his convenience. He never took Carmella on a date, but would bring over wine, and maybe they would order take-out. Carmella had decorated the bedroom with scarves and scented candles, and Emil would make love to her, slowly and expertly, watching her need and desire grow until she was begging him for the release. That was the part of any seduction that he liked most. He loved knowing that, when he was gone, she would always be wanting more of him, and would always say yes whenever he came back around.

After several weeks, Carmela received word that Joel was coming home from his deployment.

"What are we going to do?" Carmella asked beseechingly.

Emil said, "I think you should stay with my brother. He loves you and wants to marry you."

"What about us?" Carmella asked quietly.

"I won't tell him if you don't," Emil said with a shrug. And just like that, it ended.

When Joel arrived back in Miami from his tour of duty, neither Carmela nor Emil ever mentioned their affair. Emil never called or texted Carmela, and when he came over to visit, he usually had a girl with him. Joel sensed that something had happened between the two them, primarily because Carmella seemed so awkward around Emil, but there was no gossip in the family or in their circle of friends, nothing definite at all, and Joel soon became preoccupied with his work with the Hialeah Police Department.

***

Joel parked his cruiser in Catherine's driveway. The light over the front door was on, and there were lights on at the back of the duplex, which faced an open water channel.

Catherine opened the door. "Hi, again." She didn't know what else to say to him. Twenty years. Two decades. A quarter of a human life span. Were they even the same people? Catherine doubted it.

Joel took out his notebook, getting right to the business. "I forgot to ask you some questions about the stalking incident in Tampa. Specifically, can you give me a description of the man you filed a report on?"

Catherine felt light-headed. Joel. At her door. "Do you want to come in...?"

".... not...tonight. I'm still working."

Catherine shrugged to cover her embarrassment at having asked. "Tall, about 6'3". Maybe 6'4". Two hundred pounds. Dark hair, normal business cut. Light blue eyes. Good looking."

"Anything else you can tell us to help locate him, if he is in the Keys?"

"Sometimes, he had a dark sedan, like an older person's car. But he mostly drove a pickup truck in Tampa. I never noticed what specific models."

"That your vehicle?" Joel indicated Catherine's Mustang convertible.

"Yes. The woman who lives on the other side drives a motorcycle mostly."

"Thank you. Catherine. I need to get going. I'm in the middle of another investigation..."

"That's it?"

"I'll keep you updated. Keep your vehicle and your home secure."

Catherine folded her arms and twisted her lips. "Thank you, Officer."

She closed the door, poured herself a glass of cold white wine, and went out to sit on the back deck. Joel. After twenty years. Not in my wildest dreams.

The breeze had freshened, and the coconut palm tree fronds near the water rustled and scraped against one another. They make a surprising amount of noise…. or sound cover, Catherine thought.

***

"Was that her, Marco? Talking to the cop?"

"I don't know. This one looks taller, I'd say. And blonder. Just be cool."

Chapter 9
I Just Hate Being by Myself

Emil wheeled up in front of Joel and Carmela's home. He eased himself out of the Corvette. It had been a few years since he had hopped out of any low-slung vehicle. And, it had been years and years, a decade and a half or more, he couldn't recall for sure, since he and Carmella had had their time together.

They had kept their distance from each other initially, out of respect for Joel, but, over time, their relationship had evolved into a warm friendship. Carmella seemed happy with Joel, and Joel had been faithful to Carmella as far as Emil knew.

Carmella opened the door wearing a tropical print wrap skirt, nice sandals, and a casual top. Nothing too sexy, Emil noted.

"Hi, guy. Long time." She stepped back and invited him into the living room. "I have soda or wine."

"A glass of wine, thanks."

"Cheese and crackers? Or I can heat up some mini quesadillas."

"Whatever is easiest, *Chica*."

They stood together in the Florida room, gazing out at the backyard. Carmela and Joel had transformed the space from an ordinary suburban yard into a tropical oasis. The evening was still hot, but not oppressively so. Just looking at the swimming pool was refreshing.

"What's the old man up to?"

"Oh, he's down in Monroe County this evening. I guess he'll be back tomorrow or the next day. How are things with you?"

"Work is a pain in the ass. Dixon, my supervisor, is an asshole. Joel was smart to get out when he did."

"How so?"

"Same old, same old. Long hours, low pay, getting a promotion is next to impossible unless your uncle or somebody works there." Emil sighed. "All the years I've put in at the Department, and I'm still getting the short end. Dixon will never approve a promotion for me. How are things working out for Joel in the Keys?"

Carmella shrugged. "OK, I guess. He's busy on a case. The drive isn't too bad most of the time, except in tourist season or on Fridays, like that. Some nights, when he has a long shift, he stays at a place he rents."

"How are you doing with that, with him being away sometimes?"

Carmella blew out some air and picked up Coco and put the dog on her lap. "OK. I guess. I keep busy with the real estate. Market is pretty good right now. But I just hate being alone. I always have. This is almost like back when he was deployed, when he was in the Special Forces, or whatever it was."

Emil took a sip of his drink. "He's only gone two or three days at a time. So... not like the Army, really."

"I know, I know. I just hate being by myself. But I want him to be happy in his job, right?"

"Why don't you just move there?"

"It's only two or three hours, or maybe four, away, but I wouldn't see my family as much. And I like our house here. We couldn't afford a nice place like this down there. So expensive. And I like my job. Maybe he won't like his there after a while and get something back up here. That's what I hope, anyway."

Emil looked around. His gaze settled on the inviting swimming pool. "You have it good. I screwed up."

"How do you mean?" Carmella asked. They went outside and sat at down at the side of the pool, their bare feet dangling in the water.

"With Dawn, mainly. I had it good with her for ten years."

"Your longest, ever."

"By far," Emil admitted. "She had...has...a great job, head of the OR at Methodist Bay Hospital. Nice condo at the beach." He plucked a moth out of the water that had been drawn to the pool light. "She still has those things. Plus, a new doctor husband."

"Yeah, regrets," nodded Carmella.

"Tell me about it."

"You could have used a condom with Jamie."

"I hate those things."

"Maybe if you hadn't screwed around and gotten Jamie pregnant, you wouldn't now have two divorces—well, one divorce and one almost divorce-- and two kids, and all that."

"Did you know Jamie said I was getting fat? Fat and out of shape. Said that's why she left me to go back to one of her exes."

"I heard. She told me. Girls talk."

"Dennis is no prize."

"He treats her well," Carmela pointed out.

"She says she's going to marry him as soon as we get our divorce. I resent that; I really do."

"She's pregnant with his kid, Emil!"

Emil shrugged. "I just hope Joel knows what he's got and doesn't screw things up."

"What do you mean?" Carmella asked. It was fully dark now, and more bugs were being drawn to the pool light. They hit the water, and most didn't make it out of the pool. They swirled around in the current created by the pool pump, and then got sucked down into the strainers.

"Nothing. Temptation."

Carmella was silent.

"But you're probably past all that."

"Meaning?"

"Don't women stop, you know, wanting it, after they get to be in their forties?"

"Who told you that?" Carmella laughed. "We want it. Those crazy hormones are going strong."

"I just can't understand why Jamie left me."

"She was pregnant with some other guy's kid!"

"She could have had an abortion…. I would have forgiven her."

Carmella shrugged. "But would you have ever quit cheating on her?"

"She cheated on me."

"After. Only after. Women want to be able to depend on their man."

"I wish we had gotten married when we were young, back then."

"We?"

"You and me, Carmella. You really were…are…the only woman who understood who I could be. You were crazy for me."

"Don't say that. It reminds me of things I truly regret." She took a long drink of her wine.

"I'm the one with the regrets. Biggest mistake I ever made in my entire life was letting you go. I should have kept you, married you, when I had you."

"Would have, should have." said Carmella.

"Do you still love me a little?" Emil asked.

"Don't say these things. I'm married to your brother."

"Ah, yes, Saint Joel of the South Florida law enforcement community. He suffered all manner of bullshit under political bosses, but now he patrols the Overseas Highway, the soft air of the Florida Keys caressing his face."

"You're drunk."

"How about you?"

"Please go home, Emil."

"How about if I sleep it off here? Drunk driving, and all…. not a good look for a cop."

"I'll call you a taxi or an Uber."

"I love you, Carmella. I'm sorry for everything."

"Say it sober, and I might actually believe you."

Chapter 10
Across Alligator Alley

Charlie had never traveled to the Florida Keys prior to this particular trip, even though he had lived in the state since he was a child. He had spent so many years taking care of his mother as she got older and frailer, as well as working on their old house in Dade City, that he'd simply never thought about just taking the time to make the six-to-eight-hour trip. His mother hadn't been a terrible burden ever, not by any means, and the Social Security checks basically supported them both after Charlie's father died.

It was a surprise at the time to Charlie that he, too, received benefits from his late father's work record up until he graduated from high school. Almost like a reward. He had saved that money, and he and his mother lived off her widow's benefit and Charlie's part time jobs.

Then, even better, there was the good-sized life insurance policy that eventually paid off because Charlie's father had died accidentally in their garage. Mrs. Crane, the check was made out to. Charlie had simply deposited it to their joint bank account. Mother, by that time, wasn't really capable of paying attention to a lot of detail.

Since they lived pretty frugally, he was really doing okay financially, he figured. No debts, no car payments for now, and the mortgage on the house in Dade City was paid. He was a careful shopper. He figured he had enough money to support a wife, at least if they lived together in the big old Victorian in Dade City with his mother.

Of course, a wife with career interests would probably want to work. The potential problem with that was that she might meet another man and then want to leave Charlie to be with him.

He couldn't very well lock her in the basement. She wouldn't be happy down there. Possibly she could be if it were dry-walled and painted and made cozy. The plumbing for a bathroom was already there.

The miles down I-75 and across Alligator Alley passed with Charlie lost in his plans about how to make the basement in the old house livable. Part of the time, he allowed himself the thought that she would welcome the invitation to simply come home with him and live as normal people do. At other times during the long drive, he despaired of that ever happening. After all, she had run away from him all the way down to the Keys.

He had supplies in his trunk in case of either outcome. Including his mother's engagement ring. And flex cuffs. And a hood. It would be pretty much up to Catherine to decide how she wanted to play it.

Chapter 11
I'm Not Panicking

Shortly after Joel left for the second time, Kate knocked on Catherine's door.

"It's me, don't panic."

Catherine let her in. "I'm not panicking."

Kate looked her over. "Actually, you kind of look like you saw a ghost."

"I did, in a way. Turns out I know the cop who was here, from a long time ago."

"Oh yeah?" said Kate. "Do you have any wine left?"

They sat out back on the deck facing the ocean. The moonlight scattered on the rippled surface. The palms rustled and swayed in the east wind.

"Kind of late in the season for this much wind," noted Kate. "So…. what happened with the cop? Why'd he come back again?"

"Well…" Catherine began. "The first time, he looked at the dead bird. And we realized we had…met… each other before."

"And..."

"Then, he came back after a while to ask a question about the Tampa stalker."

"Do they think it's him? I knew it, I just knew it!"

"I don't know. Just covering bases, I guess."

"Do *you* think it's him?"

Catherine shrugged. "I'm not really sure."

Kate tossed her head, exasperated. "Just how many guys who leave dead things at your door decorated with ribbons do you actually think there are? We saw someone do it on purpose, on the imager. And, even if we hadn't, the ribbon makes it a near-positive ID."

Kate took a swallow of her wine and continued. "So. You have two weird things going on at once. The sea gull guy, and the old boyfriend cop, just happening to show up at your door at almost the same time."

Catherine was silent. She knew that the two occurrences were related only because Joel had randomly been the one to take the call they'd made about finding the bird on Kate's doorstep. A coincidence. But she couldn't stop thinking about him now, remembering how it had been between them, back when they were young, and life was still so fresh.

***

Joel returned to the motel scene. Paz was finished writing up the report.

"What do you think?"

"Doesn't appear to be purely a robbery. Too unusually violent. Maybe points to someone she knew, at least statistically. Cash only was taken," Paz went on. "He may be too smart to bother with stolen credit cards."

"Which leaves us with what kind of motive?"

"A guy with an excess of rage. Possibly at older women? All women? Women in bars?"

"Any similar crimes locally?"

"None reported. Most violent assaults against older women take place in nursing homes, private homes, like that. By someone she knows or is acquainted with on some level. We may have to leave this one for the Florida Department of Law Enforcement, unless we get lucky. Which would probably mean someone additional getting unlucky."

Chapter 12
Time For a Change

Joel, who had begun his law enforcement career as a sworn officer with the Hialeah, Florida police department, had, at various times, participated in State-mandated training. Sometimes, the topic of stress management was addressed, particularly the job stress that all law enforcement personnel experience over the course of their work-lives.

Some of these stressors are so common that they are essentially universal: sleep disruption and sleep disorders from night work and shift work. Encounters with death: dead bodies, dead babies, abused children. Post-traumatic stress reaction was real and common because of repeated on-the-job exposure to so much violence and the tragedies of so many human lives. The more exposure to human suffering, the more likely an officer was to develop symptoms, which often interfered with marriages and mental health.

Joel's training and discipline, first acquired from his time in an elite military unit, had generally been helpful in armoring him against some of the more disruptive symptoms police officers can develop. He understood that regular, intense, physical exercise and making priorities of physical fitness and sleep hygiene were helpful in combating the buildup of stress. Mental toughness had been taught and emphasized as much as physical strength challenges during his military training and the subsequent summer weeks and weekends with his reserve unit.

Even the most sheltered members of the general public can easily understand that near-constant exposure to death and human evil and human suffering is painful and traumatic. Less widely recognized are the negative effects of the kind of stressors that derive from the law enforcement system itself: political dealing that inserts itself where it shouldn't be a factor, the frustrating weight of the bureaucracy, and poor supervision are all root causes of stress that are at least as impactful as the daily wear and tear of the job.

Joel had learned early that thoroughly knowing the law, in terms of what he could and could not do as a sworn officer, helped counteract systemic problems like inadequate supervision. Having a strong moral code to begin with, Joel's internal compass pointed him away from the kinds of ethical compromises and opportunities for corruption that some officers were undone by. He was loyal, had some good friends, and had learned to live with the imperfections of the system and of his fellow officers. For the most part.

It troubled him that his brother Emil continued to be so vulnerable to negative influences within the department. He was relieved that, since he had joined the Monroe County Sheriff's Department, he had much less contact with Emil overall and no more contact with him whatsoever as part of the same law enforcement organization.

In his new job, Joel had to contend with a long commute and long hours. Those factors continued to interfere with his family life, and in particular, with his marriage to Carmella. He wished she would give some more consideration to moving, but he understood her love of their home and her devotion to her extended family in Kendall.

He found he was busy in Monroe, but not as crazy-busy as when he was working in Dade County. Currently, he had more traffic-related work—pileups, accidents, DUIs and speeding on the treacherous highway—than person-to-person violence.

He had been experiencing those features of the job change as actually refreshing. It was a different world from Miami-Dade, even though it was so close geographically. Much of the crime, including even traffic infractions, was committed by visitors and non-residents rather than by locals, because Monroe County and Key West were such major tourist destinations.

That, to some extent, made it harder to track criminal violators along the string of islands. They could slip in and out of the county without leaving much of a trace of their activities. A particular suspect could sometimes be tracked by the trail of their credit card purchases by a subpoena of those records...but there was no such paper trail for cash purchases. Bars, restaurants, and retail establishments kept no record of the identity of people who paid with cash. A perpetrator who was savvy about going about his business on a cash basis could easily commit at least one serious crime and go undetected...unless there were a reliable witness to the crime.... such as a victim who survived an assault.

Chapter 13
Not If I Can Help It

Charlie sat outside at the tiki bar at the Lobster Hut Motel. The night was blissfully warm, but a little humid for his taste. He looked at the women drinking and laughing. Many of the younger ones had quite a few visible tattoos. That seemed to be a local style, or maybe he was just starting to notice them since girls didn't wear too many clothes down here in the Keys. Shorts. Tank tops. Skimpy sundresses. He had been admiring a slim redhead in a yellow dress. But her arms were covered in ink. Charlie's father had had a few tattoos, an anchor and things like that from his Navy days.

Sometimes Charlie found himself missing his father. He hadn't been an altogether bad guy. He'd supported the family. He'd paid for Charlie's science fair costs and gave him money to buy electronic parts for his hobbies. He'd seemed proud of Charlie' report cards and school projects. He'd been thrifty with money and didn't have any affairs with women. Or none that Charlie had ever learned of. He did have some very dirty magazines around.

Every so often, Charlie wished his father were still alive. With him and his mother. All of them together as a family.

He really, really hoped that Catherine would come home with him. That might depend on whether or not she had found another boyfriend already. So far, all he'd seen was that cop visiting at her place for a brief while, shortly after the woman had been killed here at the Lobster Hut.

He'd also seen someone sort of staked out down the street from Catherine's place. He'd called in a description of the car and the license plate on a burner phone to a crime tip hot line. It would be a good idea if that guy could be tagged with bird or animal-killings, especially since Charlie had noticed, too late, the infrared camera set up outside Catherine's neighbor's place. The duplex arrangement had confused him.

***

Joel lay on the semi-comfortable bed at his rental unit on Grassy Key. He had found a one bedroom, one bath free-standing cottage on the bay side. The kitchen had plenty of cabinet space, but only a cook-top, a mini-fridge, and a microwave. It suited him just fine, but he doubted that Carmella would like it very much. She might like the large, screened porch facing the water. It was a pretty view.

Joel had never mentioned Catherine to Carmella, although he had, over the years, talked about other details of the trip to Mexico. He had not been dating Carmella at that point, and he had never spoken to anyone, really, about very many deeply personal details of his life once he'd joined the army.

Catherine. In Mexico, as the days passed, they'd become obsessed with each other in bed. A hundred times afterwards he'd wished he had asked for at least her address, if not her cell phone number. Back then, he'd thought he'd be too busy with his military training, part of which was all the way out in California, and she lived far away, and vacation romances aren't meant to last beyond the beach. A mistake on his part. Perhaps.

Joel thought about the stalker. Former boyfriends and former husbands were the most common offenders. Joel wondered just how much of a prior relationship Catherine had had with the man. Boyfriend? Lover? Casual acquaintance? She seemed to have implied that he was more of an acquaintance, but he couldn't be sure of that without an investigation.

Catherine could be in real danger. Under the statutes, if she had never lived with the guy, some of the protections of domestic violence legislation would probably not apply. Stalking is, however, a first-degree misdemeanor in Florida, which could potentially result in a prison term, probation, and/or a fine. A key part of the applicable statute is that an offender can be subject to a ten-year injunction, more commonly known as a restraining order.

Joel had known of a case in Miami-Dade where the injunction had been found stapled with a nail gun to the victim's dead body.

He sat up, shaken by images of Catherine's tanned body lying swathed in white sheets in their bed in Mexico superimposed with the crime photos of a case he had worked on long ago in Hialeah. A woman had been beaten to death in bed in her apartment by her ex-husband.

"She had it coming," had been the ex-husband's defense.

"Not if I can help it," he said aloud in the dark room.

Chapter 14
I Need to Know You're Going to Be Safe

Charlie made a show of leaving the Lobster Hut Motel bright and early with some beach gear and a cooler. No point in giving anyone an impression of him as anything but a happy-go-lucky vacationer. He picked up some tourist brochures from the lobby of the motel on his way out to the parking lot. He nodded to the desk clerk, whistled a cheerful tune, and put a deliberate bounce in his step.

He drove to Sombrero Beach and set up his blue beach chair and striped umbrella facing the water at the south end. Then, he went for a short swim in the warm ocean, bought an ice cream sandwich from the ice cream truck parked nearby, and sat down under the umbrella to continue his planning.

He did not need some deputy sheriff hanging around Catherine's duplex...the very last place she would ever live without Charlie by her side. He would be the one to watch over her. Take care of her. Give her what she needed. Or what she deserved.

He was taking very good care of his mother. As she became less and less able to do things for herself, he had picked up the slack. The grocery shopping. Some of the cooking. Quite a bit of the cleaning. All the yard work. She never really left the house anymore. Maybe Catherine would be the same way.

Their yard in Dade City was the best feature of the home. He had totally restored the foundation plantings with native Florida species that attracted pollinators from all over the neighborhood. Beds were fertilized and mulched. Trees were cared for as if by a professional arborist. Well, a semi-professional, Charlie conceded. He didn't really like getting up on ladders.

Everything looked very nice outside. Dozens of varieties of bromeliads grew in pots. He had some fastened to the trees.

Way in the back, there was a cemetery, not for pets or for people, but for the small animals Charlie had killed when he was much younger. Practice, he thought, it takes practice to really get your mind right about it. Some years, usually on or around Memorial Day, he went to the local cemetery where Mr. Schenck was buried. Not to pay his respects; more to stoke his memories. He hadn't been sure he'd be able to pull it off. It was a success by any standards, he thought, and one that had given him the confidence for what had to come next.

Charlie's father was buried up in Florida National Cemetery because he had been a veteran. He got a free grave site, a government headstone, and perpetual care. Charlie smiled to himself. Bushnell was less than a half-hour drive from Dade City, and he had agreed to take his mother up there whenever she wanted. Which was just once, on the first anniversary of his father's death. She had looked around, checking for other people Charlie had supposed, and then spit on his grave. Charlie smiled again at the memory. His mother was quite a woman.

He reached for his cell phone and called her. He was sure she was doing fine. He had left the house clean for her, with two weeks of groceries put away, and had reminded her which day to take out the garbage.

"Hey, ma, how are you? Are you remembering to take in the newspaper every day?" She liked to read the obituaries in the *Pasco News*.

They spoke for a while about not much of anything, and then he told her he had to go. So much for the Florida Keys sun, at least for today. He figured he had gotten enough color to make his vacation story plausible.

Next on the list: drive down to Catherine's place to find out more about who was living next door to her in the duplex. That should be easy enough. Then, learn more about that cop.

***

Catherine was awakened just after 8 am. by Joel at her door. He was out of

uniform in shorts and a white tee shirt. He'd shaved, but he looked tired.

"I didn't get much sleep. Did you?" she asked as she let him in. "Coffee?" The sun was too bright on her eastward facing deck, so they sat on the sofa inside. In the sun, she noticed the gray in his blond hair.

There was a lot of ground to cover, so much to say, so much to learn about each other's lives. Neither could find the words to begin, but they found each other's mouths, kissing the way they had in Mexico, their own personal style, mouths slightly open, his lips a little turned out so that she could lick and suck on that tender skin. Which she did, for a very long time.

Twenty years before, he would have been pushing aside her robe and welcoming her warm hand seeking his hardness. He would have readily met her need with as much as she wanted of whatever she wanted. He could feel the pulse between his legs, stuffed into his khaki shorts. He pulled back, and she met his gaze.

"You're married, aren't you," she stated flatly.

"Yes."

She waited.

"I could never forget about you."

"You didn't ask for my address or phone number when we were in Mexico."

He nodded. "I didn't think at the time it would have been fair to either one of us. I was going right into the service as soon as I got back, I didn't know what my future would be, you lived a thousand miles away, and I couldn't see it working out."

Catherine shrugged. "True enough. But. I would have felt better if you had at least asked. Even if what usually happens with a vacation romance had happened – you communicate for a while and then it fades out to maybe a Christmas card as you sink back into your daily lives."

Joel met her gaze. "I regretted it. I think back then I was just trying to save us from that, from that kind of sad way long-distance relationships always seem to fade. Speaking only for myself, leaving it like we did kept the memories of that trip perfectly encapsulated. They never got diluted by what came after."

Catherine nodded. "I understand."

He could see the questions in her eyes, and he knew what she wanted to know. So, he told her. "My wife never knew about Mexico. There was no reason to tell her, because we didn't get together until quite a while after I got back. She was in my brother's class in high school, so I vaguely knew who she was at that time, is all."

Catherine waited. What version of 'she doesn't understand me but she's a saint and I could never leave our kids' was he going to come up with? But he didn't say anything more.

"My husband died of cancer two years ago, and I don't have children. Just him." She indicated Rocky, who had climbed up on her lap.

Joel nodded. "My wife is in real estate and doesn't want to move down here at this point. I go back up to Kendall on my days off. I'll be leaving for three days after my shift tonight, or tomorrow morning at the latest." He stood up to go. "I need to know that you're going to be safe."

They stepped outside together and walked over to Joel's patrol car.

"Safe from Charlie, or whoever it is?" Catherine smiled with that little twist that she sometimes made with her lips. That mouth. Joel reached out and pulled her to him again and kissed her for a long time. She pressed herself to his body, enjoying a small sense of triumph as she felt him stiffen against her.

Chapter 15

After Mexico

Joel left, and Catherine sat with Rocky for a while. Her body was buzzing, and she was flooded with her memories.

After Mexico, she had stepped right into a new job. Had taken up a daily yoga practice. Jumped into a different, vibrant social scene which had led to new romances and friendships.

One night, about three months after she'd gotten back, she was in her bed, alone, and the moon was casting a little silver light through her bedroom curtains. This was up North, before she had moved to Tampa. It was in late November, around the time of Joel's birthday, and she wondered if, right now, wherever he was in the world, he could be looking up at that same quarter moon and thinking about her.

The next time Catherine thought about Joel was a whole year later, soon after she'd moved to Tampa. She imagined him being somewhere just across the state from her, barely two hundred miles away as the crow flies. But he had said he was joining the Army, or something. He could be anywhere in the world at this point. She thought about trying to find his mother's telephone number and asking her how to reach him. What stopped her was remembering that he hadn't asked for her address when he could have, while they were standing by the taxi in Cozumel that was ready to take him to the airport and out of her life.

After that, her days and weeks and months and years were so full and so busy that, when she thought about diving in Cozumel or walking around the archaeological site at Chichen-Itza, Joel crossed her mind barely, if at all. Eventually, she had married, happily so.

That was then. Now, though, she was awash with her memories and sensations and doubts. He was married. She was a widow. Her emotions were perhaps in a more precarious state than his. "I will keep myself safe and protected," she said softly, like a yoga affirmation to reassure the vulnerable parts of her heart. "Also, I need to get ready to go to work," she told Rocky, who blinked in the sun.

Chapter 16
A Terrier with An Old Sock

Marco tossed a regulation Little League baseball to his kid in their back yard in Key West, thinking about what had happened up the Keys. Sweat had already darkened his gray tee-shirt, but the boy looked as fresh as a daisy, he noted. Kids have nothing to worry about, because they don't even know what's ahead of them. They're like dogs in that way, up to a certain age. Then they wise up to the ways of the world. Which is probably why kids can just be so happy.

He might not be after tonight's tryouts. Kid wanted to pitch for the Little Conchs, but there were two better boys ahead of him in the rotation. No harm in letting him imagine success for a while. Plus, because of restricted pitch count allowances, the kid would probably get his chance from time to time.

Marco had finally tracked down Miss Kelly Ann Morrison. Very successfully, he had told Olivera. She had no idea she'd been ID'd, he sniggered. Although it was looking more and more like she'd forgotten what she had seen at the Blue Oyster or had never actually understood what had gone down there, even though she seemed to have been looking right at it. Still, it was hard for him to let it go. Olivera had said he was like a terrier with a smelly old sock.

It had been a mildly interesting stake-out, from down the street. The cop. The other girl. Plus, the guy in the car watching the place, too. Big guy, dark hair, older model sedan. Had been hanging around the area more than Marco himself.

This particular cop appeared to be more focused on the other side of the duplex. Olivera was worked up for nothing. Chick hadn't seen a thing down at the Blue Oyster or else cared nothing about what she had seen.

The cop had spent twenty, thirty minutes in there this morning. Maybe he was plowing the blonde.

Marco had yawned. A waste of time. He'd tell Olivera to just let it ride. Nothing was happening here that related to them. Time to move on.

He had been thinking about pulling out from his parking spot in the shade of some tall Ixora to maybe get a coffee, when the blonde had come out dressed for work, got into the red Mustang, and drove off. The other chick's motorcycle was still parked.

Marco had still been thinking about his next move when the guy in the older sedan took off, wheels kicking up gravel. He turned north on the Overseas Highway, the same direction the blonde had taken. Of course, there were only two choices on that road.

He had stared off into the distance, considering.

"Hey!" The chick he was supposed to be watching was right there, pounding on his roof. "What the hell are you hanging around here for? I know what you're up to, buddy.

Get your ass back to Tampa. The cops here know all about your sick little game!"

Marco had sped off, his tires spinning in a cloud of coral dust. Tampa? What the fuck was he going to tell Olivera? The chick was flat-out nuts.

"Dad!" his kid yelled. "I've got three more pitches to throw!"

Chapter 17
What Is He Up To?

As Joel headed up the Overseas Highway at the end of his shift, he found himself driving more and more slowly. He could see the line of cars piled up behind him in his rear-view mirror. If he hadn't been in the Monroe County vehicle, the honking drivers and the crazy passing that contribute to this highway's death toll would have roused him before this. But not many people would crazy-pass a cop car.

He wasn't really tired. He was merely oblivious to some of the most spectacular ocean scenery in the country because his thoughts were with Catherine and assessing the risk that she might face from the stalker. As much as he personally wanted to protect her, he would not be nearby for days at a time, and when he was at work, his shift might take him as far as fifty miles away, at least for parts of each day.

It was difficult to tell what Charlie was really up to. Most romantically rejected stalkers fall into some kind of a loose category. Was he an intimacy-seeking stalker? More likely, based on Catherine's efforts to separate herself from him, going so far as to move four hundred miles away only to be followed, Charlie might be more of a classic rejected stalker. Restraining orders usually are interpreted by this type as more evidence of rejection, so getting one can drive up the risk. If the dead animals were "gifts" or threats from Charlie, or both, he was probably a rejected stalker-type. A pretty crazy one.

What did he really want? Did he simply want a relationship with Catherine? Did he want to punish her, maybe kill her, for rejecting him? Was he prepared for either possibility?

Joel wondered about Charlie's past, particularly any history of violence he might have. Apparently, Catherine had been very clear with Charlie that she did not want a relationship with him, but he had followed her all the way to the Keys.

Was he intending to make another plea for a relationship? If so, why hadn't he directly contacted her? Leaving a dead bird at the doorstep wasn't really much of a romantic gesture, assuming that that had been his little gift. Catherine had certainly thought it fit his pattern.

Did he have an abduction in mind? Rape? Murder?

As he made his way up the Keys toward home, Joel placed two calls. The Tampa police department confirmed that a patrol vehicle had been sent to Catherine Cameron's Tampa address within the past sixty days, and that there had been a verbal warning issued to a Charles Crane. No further action.

Next, he called an old friend from his reserve unit, Dave, who was now with the sheriff's department in Pasco County.

Deputy Sheriff David Raspin agreed to review any reports or other relevant information, and to talk to Charlie's mother right away.

The coroner's report on Charlie's father's death wasn't very detailed, as it turned out, but it indicated cause of death was a traumatic head injury preceded by an accidental fall in the deceased's garage.

Sheriff Raspin drove his patrol car out to the Crane place. It took several minutes before Charlie's mother appeared at the door. She was in a house dress and slippers but looked to be in good health. She stared at Sheriff Raspin, who tipped his hat to her.

"Is this about the insurance?" she asked timidly. "I told Charlie...." She caught herself and didn't say anything more.

"No, nothing about insurance," Raspin said jovially. "Just looking in on you - a welfare check-up."

"Did Charlie send you? I told him I'm fine. He's on a trip somewhere."

"No, he didn't. I heard he was away, and I'm just seeing if you need anything. He's in the Keys, did you say?"

"I didn't say that," Mrs. Crane snapped, her mood shifting. "I have plenty of food, and he'll be back home soon. Maybe tonight."

"Okay, ma'am, just give a call if you need anything." He handed her his card.

"Deputy Sheriff David Raspin," she read aloud. "Why are you here, did you say? Charlie's not here..." Her eyes had developed a vague, confused look.

"Sorry to have troubled you." Raspin left.

She seemed like a mildly confused elderly woman trying to put up a facade of competence but who, instead, came across as fragile and fearful. She really shouldn't be left alone. Raspin wondered what her son was up to that was important enough to leave her by herself.

Chapter 18
We Can't Change the Past

Joel arrived home in good time, despite Friday afternoon traffic, and greeted Carmella with a kiss and a hug. She smelled wonderful and was dressed for dinner.

He smiled, trying to hide his exhaustion. "You look all ready. I'm going to take a quick shower and change clothes."

***

At work, Catherine was busy enough to keep her mind off Joel, but at home that evening, she felt a wave of sadness. It had been both shocking and very exciting to reconnect with Joel so suddenly out of nowhere. She had never expected to see him again and had made her peace with that years ago.

More than a decade, in fact, had passed without him ever crossing her mind. She had met, fallen in love with, and married a terrific man, and had had a good life until the lung cancer diagnosis suddenly ripped their warm cocoon apart. He had died nine months after he was diagnosed, nearly to the day.

For Catherine, the fog and the pain of being a new widow was devastating, but she had never had much faith that her husband would survive, from the first time he'd coughed up the blood. She had used the library at the university where she worked to scour medical journals and found nothing to support any hope.

Her husband, though, was an optimistic man, and really never considered that his illness was terminal. Catherine supported him emotionally through surgery, chemotherapy, and radiation treatments as his health failed, even as he kept conveying his positive outlook to friends and family who lived at a distance. Catherine encouraged his sister and brother-in-law to come visit at Christmas. As soon as they saw him, his sister's face told Catherine that she at last understood that her brother was dying.

The funeral took place not long after on a bright Tampa Saturday morning. Catherine wore an ivory silk suit and listened carefully to the friends who spoke about what her husband's life had meant to them. It was a beautiful service, and she was thankful so many people had come to show how much they had cared about him.

She went home alone, barely able to breathe, and started on her long journey of figuring out how to go on living, feeling as if her heart had been ripped out of her body.

She survived her grief, and over time, moved out from under its weight.

Reconnecting with Joel, a married Joel whose kisses had stirred her body and her heart, was emotionally treacherous for her. As much as she wanted more of him, a lot more, she was determined to avoid the pain that would be inevitable if she fell in love with him. He wasn't available, and she would not be a married man's secret from his wife. She'd been through enough.

***

Carmella kept snatching quick looks at Joel over their plates of pasta. In the low light of the restaurant, his eyes were cast in shadows. He ate his food slowly and was drinking more wine than he usually did. She reached her hand out across the table and touched his arm.

"Are you OK, Cariño?"

"I'm sorry. Still thinking about work. How did things turn out with the listing you showed?"

Carmela shrugged. "They seemed a little interested. Lots of inventory in the area. The seller might have to make some price concessions to move it."

Joel nodded, his mind already elsewhere. Carmela wondered if Joel knew that Emil had been coming around again. She decided to confront her concerns.

"Heard you from your brother lately?"

"No. Why? Have you?"

Wrong move. She shouldn't have raised the topic. Now she would have to tell him something true. Joel could always, always tell a lie.

"Yeah, he came over the other evening for a while. We talked about kids we went to school with back in the day."

"How's he doing?"

"OK, I guess. He sounded like he wishes he was still with Dawn."

Joel shrugged. "We can't change the past, even if we want to. Just do the best we can, from here on."

Carmella dropped her eyes. What did he mean? Was he trying to tell her something?

Chapter 19
Why The Flex Cuffs?

Marco pulled out onto the Overseas Highway headed south, tires squealing.

Fuck, fuck, fuck.

No one was following him, he determined after a few miles, so he pulled in to the Lobster Hut on the right to calm down. A few beers would help.

He sat at the outside bar, checking his phone. He ordered a beer, and then another one. It wasn't happy hour, so he had to pay full price, but he didn't care about that right now.

Why wasn't Olivera answering? Had he lost his cool again about something? Like *he* had anything to worry about when, as usual, Marco was the one taking all the heat. That crazy chick.

Why am I the one who has to do all the dirty work, take all the risks? I've got stuff to take care of. Does he expect me to pop her in broad daylight?

He was halfway through his second beer, when two sheriff's vehicles pulled into the parking lot, lights flashing.

Marco looked around to check for possible escape routes. He got up, casually tossed a twenty on the table, and headed in the direction of the restrooms. A glance over his shoulder told him all he needed to know about where they were headed.

Fuck.

Marco managed to keep his cool somewhat and slid behind some lobster traps that were piled up six to eight feet behind the small building where the restrooms were located. The stench from the traps was nauseating. These were freshly pulled traps, so the tiny ocean water flora and fauna that had attached themselves to the wood slats while the traps were resting on the sea floor awaiting their lobster guests were now decomposing in the sun.

Miserably, he sank to the ground, careful not to tip over the pile of traps. He decided to wait until it was dark, and then go home.

If he wasn't in jail by then.

***

Charlie sat at the bar at the Lobster Hut, nursing a rum and Diet Coke. He didn't want to be fat when he finally had Catherine in his arms again. They were a perfect couple just the way they were.

He watched the cops who had pulled up, a couple of whom were casually making their way around the bar. Locals who knew them, from back in school maybe, nodded. Charlie just ignored them, his eyes on one of the television screens. Like he cared about either the Marlins or the Rays. He'd never played sports as a kid. Some kids had fathers who played ball with them, but his never had.

Charlie wasn't the least bit concerned that the police might be looking for whoever had taken the dead lady's cash the other night. He was one hundred percent sure no one would think it was him. He was just an ordinary Keys tourist, dressing and acting the part perfectly.

The band started playing their set. They did fairly good versions of Jimmy Buffet tunes and *Sailing*, Charlie thought. Classic Keys bar music.

***

Joel found he didn't have much of an appetite. He picked at some conch fritters. Carmela kept looking at him nervously, he thought. By the time their main courses arrived, Joel could no longer suppress his multiplying concerns about Catherine being alone down in the Keys with a possible stalker targeting her while he was up in Miami at dinner.

He excused himself from the table and called Paz. Paz agreed to watch the duplex where Catherine lived and took down the information about the vehicles Joel reported as having been seen in her area.

"I'll get over there whenever I can. In between traffic stops and dispatch calls," he assured Joel.

***

How to deal with that girl living next to Catherine? Charlie mused. She sure was a nosy one. Reminded him of some of the neighbor ladies when he was growing up.

Of course, they hadn't had actual surveillance set-ups on the perimeters of their property the way this girl did. Not that they really needed anything fancy, because they were always peering out of their windows. As if they knew things about Charlie. Maybe they did. Charlie stopped seeing any of their pets outside in their yards after a while. Cats would have been harder to catch than little dogs. He never had bothered with cats. He kind of liked them. They were good hunters, good killers. Some of those dogs had been real yappers. Until they weren't. Eventually, the only times he ever saw any little dogs was when they were getting walked on a leash. Most of those old ladies were gone now. Charlie had had absolutely nothing whatsoever to do with any of them dying. Not even his mother had been suspicious.

Speaking of which, time to call her again and see how she was doing.

"Hi, Ma," he said into his cell phone as he made his way to his car. "How are you?"

"There was a police officer here. I don't know what he wanted. He said he was doing a check up on me."

"What kind of a checkup? What did you tell him?"

"That you were on a trip and would be home soon. When are you coming back?"

Charlie hesitated. As much as he wanted to take Catherine home with him as soon as he possibly could, it might be getting a little too risky temporarily for that part of his plan. Impulsively, he said, "Tonight. I'll be back very late tonight. Leave the lights on out front and in the hall, so I don't disturb you. And remember, we don't have to worry about the electricity bill."

He didn't bother to check out of his room at the motel. This time of year, it could be very difficult to find another reasonably priced place to stay in the Keys. He'd be back in a day or two to finish his business. He still had the room reserved for a few more days, so he left some of his things, messed up the bed and a few of the towels, and put down a nice tip for the maid. Since he was paying cash for the room, he paid ahead for a few more days on his way out. No credit card trails, no formal record of his stay. Unless you considered the fake ID he'd used to check in a formal record.

He decided to do just one more drive-by of Catherine's duplex before he headed off the island chain to go calm his mother down. No real plan—he just needed to feel close to Catherine for a little while before he left.

Paz watched the sedan slow as it cruised down Catherine's street and doubled back. It stopped two houses away for a few minutes, and then headed out to US 1 heading north. Paz followed discretely for a mile or two and put on his flashers as soon as the vehicle exceeded the speed limit.

"Driver's license, registration, sir," Paz said when Charlie lowered his window.

"May I ask why I'm being stopped?" Charlie handed Paz the documentation.

"Do you know what the speed limit is here?"

"Fifty-five," said Charlie. "Which is what I was doing. Sir."

"Not here. Forty-five miles an hour in this area."

"Sorry."

"Please step out of the vehicle and open the trunk."

Charlie complied. Paz saw a small overnight bag. Some rope. A blanket. And some disposable plastic hand cuffs. About twenty dollars for twenty-five of them. Not illegal, but questionable.

"You are visiting Monroe County from Pasco County?"

"Yes. Having a great time. I'm going to be proposing to my girlfriend down here in a few days."

"Why the flex cuffs?"

"In case she says 'no'," Charlie joked. "But seriously, I have an engagement ring. Want to see it?"

Paz had no legal reason to hold Charlie, but he made note of the license plate number and Charlie's driver's license number.

"Drive safely and watch your speed along here."

He called Joel right away with the update.

Chapter 20

Not This Guy

Joel lay awake, thinking about Catherine and Charlie. He was exhausted from his emotionally challenging week, but he was fighting off his need for sleep until he felt he had more of a handle on Charlie's motivation and intentions.

Carmella had fallen asleep right away, as soon as her head hit the pillow. He hadn't thought she would, that maybe she would want to talk, because she had seemed so anxious most of the evening. Maybe it was all the wine she drank at dinner.

Paz had reported there was an engagement ring and flex cuffs in Charlie's car, and that he said he was going home to Pasco County.

What did Charlie have in mind? Paz said he had stated that he was going to propose to his girlfriend. Truth or lie? A girlfriend in the Keys or one in Pasco? Could the girlfriend be Catherine?

The combination of flex cuffs and a diamond ring was disturbing. If Charlie was obsessive enough to have tracked Catherine all the way to the Keys, nothing was off the table.

Joel tried to imagine himself in Charlie's situation. A lonely single guy, an attractive widow. They knew each other, had had some interaction. How much? Catherine could be minimizing. Had they been lovers? Had she broken his heart? Didn't matter. Stalking and kidnapping were illegal, and more than that, crazy in this situation.

What did Charlie intend? Could he be planning to murder her? Joel wished he had more detail on Charlie's history from his friend, David Raspin, up in Pasco. Too late at night to call him again now.

Charlie's kind of behavior did not just appear in someone's repertoire without a significant history of priors, whether or not there was a record. It was planned and deliberate, not an impulsive act. No one could drive four hundred miles without having second thoughts, no matter how upset and agitated they were when they first set out. Joel's eyelids fluttered and closed...Paz will watch Catherine's place...and Joel was out.

***

Marco must have fallen asleep under the lobster traps. It was getting near dark, and it was raining. Drops of water, fouled by the traps, dripped on to his face and hair. Disgusting. Someone is going to have to pay for this.

He crawled out from under the pile, feeling in his pants for his car keys. He looked around, and decided to head straight for his vehicle, whether it was being watched or not. A night in jail would be better than another minute under the wet, smelly mountain of wood.

He was almost inside his vehicle, when, damn, they nailed him.

The deputy walked him over to the bar for the server to identify.

"Not this guy. No way. The guy who was here was tall and good-looking."

She wrinkled her nose and walked away.

You'd smell, too, honey, if you'd spent any time under those traps, Marco thought. He waited for the deputy to make up his mind about what to do with him.

The deputy ran his ID, and since Marco was pretty sure he had nothing outstanding, it seemed he would get turned loose. Just another Keys drunk, sleeping it off in a public place.

The deputy made a call and turned back to Marco.

"This vehicle has been reported on more than one occasion recently, parked on East Circle Drive. Can you explain your purpose for being there?"

Marco was tempted to give one of the smart-ass answers that came to mind. But he was cold, wet, and stinking, and did not want to spend the night in jail. So, he admitted that he sometimes parked his car in the shade there to nap, on his way to or from Key West. Nothing more than that.

"Know anyone on that street? Why there?"

"No, Officer, but I did some landscaping work last season for a guy who was selling his house there. So, I feel safe in the area." What a joke.

Marco had a small record of petty crimes, but nothing that would warrant holding him. The jails and detention facilities would probably get crowded with Friday night arrests. The deputy let him go with an admonition to stay out of places where he had no business.

Once he was on the road, the first call Marco made was to Olivera. His cell phone battery was dangerously low, but he didn't worry about that. When he was finally through venting, he had made up his mind to make that bitch pay. Which one, he wasn't sure. Maybe both of them. All of them. Everyone.

Chapter 21
Lock Your Doors

Marco cleaned himself up at the outdoor showers at Sombrero Beach and changed into a pair of khaki shorts and a tee shirt he had in the car. He left the foul-smelling clothes he'd been wearing in one of the beach trash containers. He then drove to the duplex to make someone pay for everything he'd gone through so far today.

It was pitch black already when he arrived. He parked down the street. The wind was kicking up from the east. Marco sat and drank the beer he'd bought on the way. All that time under the stinking lobster traps, all because he was afraid of going back to jail for a very long time. First degree they couldn't make stick, but second degree they might. Olivera's kid would either have to go in to foster care or to one of his depraved relatives. Kid's mother wouldn't get out of Lowell Correctional for another year or more. Kid should be with his family.

Unless that family was like his own had been. Total losers. Marco hated to even think about his childhood. He'd admired Wolverine, the Ninja Turtles, all of that kind of thing, just like any other boy of his generation. No one who raised him had any redeeming qualities whatsoever. Possibly except his Uncle Ryan. He'd finished high school, gone into the Army, and died in Iraq.

Marco got out of his car. He walked down to the duplex, and, keeping to the shadows cast by the shifting palm branches, made his way to the ocean side. From the street, the right side of the duplex was dark; a light was on in the left side unit. There was enough moonlight for him to make his way around to the waterfront without tripping over the pile of beach gear that one of those bitches had left out.

Kate, on her cell phone in her dark apartment, quietly said, "I'm picking up someone right outside. Lock your doors. Call the cops."

The sliding glass door was open. A Siamese cat was staring out at him through the screen. The blonde was on her cell phone. The cat hissed and arched its back. The blonde got up and stared into the darkness through the screen. She shut and locked the slider, and then went to the front door and locked it.

Marco cursed silently. It was the wrong girl. The one he wanted must be on the other side. This was the one who'd been boinking the cop.

Marco stood on is tiptoes and peered into the open bathroom window on the other side. He could see the one he wanted walking around, talking on her cell phone. He slipped around to the back and tried her slider again. Locked. Unless he wanted to try kicking it in, he would have to wait until she fell asleep and then jimmy it.

He decided to just sit down in the dark and rest for a while. Too much action today. The moonlight sparkled on the ocean. The breeze was up. It would keep the bugs away. He might even take a nap, just for a minute or two.

Marco was awakened by a bright light in his face. Two Monroe County deputies lifted him to his feet by his armpits, cuffed him, and half-dragged, half-carried him to their patrol car. Fuck.

Catherine stepped outside and motioned to Paz.

She whispered, "Can you ask him about the dead bird that was left at the door the other day?"

Marco looked slightly surprised at the question. "I don't know anything about a dead bird. I don't like birds. They shit all over my car. I'm sure as hell not touching one."

His anger had dissipated. He was looking at another arrest, one that might well result in the cops connecting him with the shrimper's death. He decided to play the role of a simple Keys drunk. Wouldn't be that far of a stretch, he thought.

It seemed that the cops might be willing to buy it.

"I'm really sorry I frightened her; I was just looking at the water in the moonlight. Then I fell asleep. Maybe I shouldn't have been on the property. I didn't mean any harm."

Kate, standing near Catherine in the shadows, whispered, "That's the guy. One of the ones I saw in Key West at the shrimp docks bar." She took a deep breath, and stepped forward and said firmly, "Officer. I'm pretty sure this is the man who stabbed a guy down at the Blue Oyster in Key West last month. He's apparently been skulking around here ever since. If I'd realized it was him, I would have said something a long time ago."

When Kate's parents found out that their daughter had been a possible witness to a murder at one of Key West's seedier waterfront bars and had delayed reporting it, they immediately hired a lawyer and whisked Kate away to Tallahassee.

The limo they'd sent to take her to the airport sat idling in the driveway of the duplex while Kate hugged Catherine goodbye.

"I don't know when I'll be able to come back here, but I will. My parents are going to need some time to get calmed down, I think.

All my imaging equipment is at your disposal, but I have to take my laptop, so you'll need to hook it up to yours. I'll text you instructions."

"Maybe it was only ever your guys around here. I was so scared that Charlie had followed me to the Keys...now, I wonder if I was wrong...maybe I over-reacted."

Kate thought for a moment. "Well, what about the bird? The ribbon? Not my guys' *modus operandi*. That's your guy's thing, right? Don't let your guard down!"

"Something else could have killed the bird..."

"It was wearing a ribbon, Catherine, remember? Be careful! Get that cop you know to help keep you safe until they can nail the bird-killer."

The limo pulled out of the driveway and turned left toward the Key West airport. Catherine felt more alone than she had since right after her husband had died. Her only friend in the Keys was gone. Joel was up in Miami with his wife. She picked up her cat, Rocky, and hugged him.

Chapter 22
Sunday Morning

Sunday morning, Catherine went out to try to make herself feel better with a beach yoga class at the Marathon Community Park. She made sure Rocky was secure in the apartment, took her yoga mat, strap, and blocks, and left for what she hoped would be a morning of a strengthening and calming discipline.

After, she went to her job at the Sparkling Tarpon. It was a quiet afternoon shift. She didn't make much money in tips. When she returned home, Rocky was in the kitchen window, waiting for her. Everything seemed undisturbed inside. Catherine thought about fiddling with the imagining device Kate had left for her but decided to try to go to sleep early instead. She was having a hard time shaking off her blue mood.

She wondered if Joel was thinking about her, too, as he lay in bed with his wife.

Chapter 23
Her Name Is Catherine

Charlie woke up after his long drive home to Dade City from the Keys feeling...what? Sad? Angry? Hopeful? Sometimes, no matter how hard he thought about it, he could not figure out what he felt. Often, it was a mix of two contradictory emotions: relieved/angry; loving/scared; frightened/thrilled.

He got out of his bed in the room he'd had all through his childhood and adolescence. And now, adulthood. He'd never lived on his own, except for college, and even then, he'd been in a dormitory with the other boys.

When he'd come back home after college, it was because his widowed mother was getting a little too afraid to be by herself. That's what he told other people. In truth, she had badgered him in to coming back, and insisted he wouldn't be able to get a good enough job, or pay his bills, or take care of himself.

Sometimes, he got so angry with her that he wanted to hit her. Nothing he ever did was quite enough. Her tea wasn't sweet enough. Did he buy the right kind of detergent, the kind that didn't make her skin break out in hives? Today was Wednesday, don't forget, they had to change their bedding today.

Mostly, he barely paid any attention to her string of complaints.

He didn't recall her being so vocal about her many dissatisfactions back when he was a kid. Maybe it was because she had been afraid Charlie's father would hit her if she said anything. When he had died, it was like she could safely start to complain about things, and she hadn't shut up since.

They sat together out on the wide veranda that faced the back yard and drank their tea. A flock of Osceola wild turkeys had wandered onto the lawn. They pecked at insects and whatever else they liked to eat. Charlie imagined Catherine sitting next to him, enjoying some herbal tea.

"Why are the police looking for you?" his mother finally asked.

"What did you tell them?"

"Nothing. You left me alone to take a trip, and you were coming back soon. And you did," she said with satisfaction.

"What, exactly, did they say they wanted, Mother?"

"Oh, I don't know. It's hard to remember. He wasn't very clear about why he was here. He asked where you were, like I told you. That's all, really."

"Well, did you? Tell him where I was?"

"No. I told you. No."

"Try to remember exactly what the policeman said."

"Was he a policeman?" Mrs. Crane looked confused. He was losing her. She was drifting off into that fog that enveloped her sometimes. People attributed it to her age, but Charlie remembered her as always tending to fade out when a situation or conversation turned unpleasant.

Maybe it was hereditary.

Or maybe living with Charlie's father had done it to both of them.

"Did Dad ever hit you?" Charlie couldn't remember ever seeing it, but it could have happened when he wasn't around, or when he was too young to process what he was seeing.

She looked up, startled by the question. "A long time ago, once or twice maybe, before you were even born."

Charlie thought she was confabulating, but he went along with it. As long as they were having this discussion, he asked, "Why didn't you ever do anything to stop him when he was beating me?"

Tears, a surprise, welled up in his eyes and spilled over onto his cheeks. He wiped them away.

"Oh, I don't think he ever really hit you, did he? I never saw it."

Charlie stood up, towering over the shrunken old lady.

"He beat me within an inch of my life. You used to put ice packs on my face and my body. Was that to keep Social Services from finding out that we were living with a monster?"

"He had a temper. Some men do," she quavered.

"You spit on his grave, Mother. I saw you do it."

"Did I? I don't think I would do something like that…"

Charlie took a deep breath. Stay calm. It doesn't matter. The monster is dead. There were more important things to talk about. He sat back down.

"Mother, I need to tell you something. Quite soon, I am going to bring home my bride, and she'll be living with us from now on. Her name is Catherine. I think you'll like her."

"Charlie, it sounds like you're imagining things again. When you were a little boy, you used to talk about flying to the moon in a spaceship. You wanted to be an astronaut."

"And you told me it would never happen, Mother. Only this really is going to happen. Her name is Catherine. She's real. I'm going to give her your diamond engagement ring from Dad."

"What a piece of luck that'll be."

The old lady laughed. Was it a mean laugh or a nervous, frightened laugh? Charlie couldn't always tell with her.

"You're more than forty years old, Son. It's too late for a wife. This is something you should have thought about when you were younger."

"She'll be here in a few more days. I think she'll be a little shy at first, so I'll probably keep her in my room until she calms down."

116

Mrs. Crane laughed again. It *was* an ugly laugh, or, again, maybe a frightened laugh. Not a happy laugh. Catherine had a happy laugh.

"You'll have to tie her up to keep her here, won't you, Son? What kind of woman would ever want to live with you? You can't hold a job. And you never had the gumption to stand up to your father, did you?"

Charlie's face turned red with rage. His fingers twitched. He stepped back, fighting an urge to choke her to death.

His mother knew damn well what he was capable of. She just like to pretend that she didn't.

Catherine...she would find out, too, soon enough.

Chapter 24
It Was a Long Time Ago

Catherine read the instructions Kate had sent her and set up the imaging equipment so that the feed would run through her own laptop. Kate had shown her how to create a personalized sound alert. Catherine chose a ping that she liked. Now, every time a stray cat or a delivery driver came anywhere within a few feet of the perimeter of the duplex, she would know. At least she would if she were awake or awakened. She increased the volume level a bit.

Rocky waited for her to come and sit back down on the couch. Then he curled up on her lap.

Outside, it was cloudy, and the water was choppy. The persistent east wind kept the palm trees swaying. Catherine started to doze with the warm cat, dreaming about the swells at the Chankanaab reef off Cozumel that had rocked her and swayed her gently under the water.

Joel was nearby, examining a lobster hole in the reef. Trigger fish schooled past them. It was a long time ago, and life's difficulties had not seemed very near. In the dream, they were much younger and a little bit sunburned, and it was in a time when there was nothing to keep them from each other.

Then, he disappeared without waving goodbye, and she surfaced, almost out of air, her head barely above the waves.

Catherine woke. Her mouth was dry. Rocky was warm on her lap. Joel was ninety-nine miles away with his wife.

Chapter 25

When They'd All Been Younger

Joel's parents had stayed together, maybe not in love, but definitely partners in life, until his father had died of a heart attack when Joel was sixteen. His old man had been all of forty-seven.

Joel picked up cash in high school at whatever part time jobs he could find. That and Social Security for him and his brother, and their mother's wages, had kept them afloat until Emil graduated from high school and Joel enlisted in the Marines.

He'd initially chosen the Marines for what he later admitted to himself was something of a young man's fantasy. After he'd developed a more realistic concept of where his opportunities and talents lay, he'd transferred to the Army Special Forces. The physical and emotional challenges of the training amplified his natural confidence and mental toughness, which later helped him make a successful career transition into law enforcement.

Joel was better equipped for police work than a majority of people who choose to enter the academy. He was already physically and mentally seasoned from his time in the military. He was clear within himself about which side of the law he wanted to be on. His internal moral compass tended to propel him away from situations and choices that were tempting trip-ups to some others in his field.

He'd pressed himself to do a good job for his community, and to shrug off the many contradictions and frustrations of the job. His reward, as he saw it, after two decades, was career longevity, a good reputation, and a degree of financial security.

Could he do what the job required of him in Monroe County? Could he protect Catherine and still be true to his marriage vows? This time, his moral compass wasn't settling in a clear direction.

***

Carmella woke up with a slight headache and a dry mouth. Too much wine last night. Joel was already up. She brushed her teeth and dressed in a nice outfit, one that flattered her curves. They hadn't made love last night. Did she want to? Did he want to?

She found him in the living room on his lounge chair staring off into space. She recognized the look—he was thinking hard about a case. She saw that his coffee cup was nearly empty and made him a fresh one the way he liked it. Life with a cop.

Joel was, in fact, was thinking about Catherine's stalker case, but he was also feeling guilty.

He had kissed an old girlfriend. He had wanted to do much more than that. He hadn't felt so much desire for a woman for a long time.

It wouldn't make anything in his marriage better if he told Carmella. She would worry every time he left for work. She would want to know details. She might insist on meeting Catherine so she could assure herself that her worries were unfounded. More likely, she would do her own Internet background check, and then really start to worry.

There were probably photos of Catherine online somewhere, and if there were, Carmella would find them. Catherine still looked beautiful. She had been a pretty young girl, but she'd grown up to be a beautiful mature woman. Carmella would feel she couldn't compete with a tall, slender blonde. Which was ridiculous, because there was absolutely no competition. Catherine was simply a woman he had known decades ago for a short time who was now the possible target of a stalker. Carmella was his wife. He had always been faithful.

If he were being absolutely honest with himself, however, Joel would admit that he couldn't easily let go of the feelings that being with Catherine had reignited. Their kisses troubled him less than the feelings. Joel kissed and hugged Carmela's cousins when they all got together. Other women, too. Now and then, he ran in to an old girlfriend. None of that meant anything, and he knew that Carmella understood. She could be quite the flirt in her own way, and he had never minded.

Interesting that she kept the wattage of her charm turned down so low around his brother. Many women, husbands present or not, pushed themselves to the front of the crowd to get Emil's attention--a quick hug, or a kiss on the tops of their heads. Maybe more so back when they had all been younger.

Long ago, Joel had participated in some counseling sessions after he'd been forced to shoot a suspect during an arrest scenario gone bad. Internal Affairs had cleared him. He had followed procedures. But he'd still felt guilty. The guy he'd shot had been young and stupid, with two little kids.

Joel second-guessed the choices he had made at the scene and slept poorly. He missed some days at work. He drank. His supervisor at the time suggested that he voluntarily get counseling, rather than referring him for a formal fitness-for-duty evaluation. The counseling sessions helped Joel accept that the feelings resulting from the outcomes of that awful situation were just feelings. Nothing had to be done because of feelings. Most of the time, maybe, feelings should be just felt, and experienced for what they can teach us, rather than acted upon.

He should be capable of behaving like the experienced law enforcement professional that he was. He could still do everything in his power to protect Catherine—as he would for any citizen at risk—without destroying his marriage. After Catherine was no longer in danger, they could be...what? Friends? Acquaintances with a past?

Joel had had lots of law enforcement experience doing exactly the right thing but then sometimes finding that he had mixed feelings about the outcome. The Catherine situation seemed like it was going to be one of those.

I could never forget about you, he thought. And I don't have to. But that's as far as it's going to go.

Doing the right thing should feel better than it actually did.

Chapter 26
Charlie Has a Girl

Joel sat in his brown leather recliner with his feet up. The bright Miami sun splashed across the swimming pool in the back yard where Carmela was reclined on a plush pool float talking on her phone. Joel rotated his chair away from the view and thought about what he had learned from a recent call from Dave, his law enforcement contact in Pasco County.

Dave had re-confirmed that Charlie's father's death long ago had been officially attributed to a fall on a concrete garage floor. The county had not flagged the death as suspicious at the time, in part because of the man's age and the fact that falls are a leading cause of death in older adults.

A company known for its stringent claims examination protocol had made a substantial life insurance payout.

Those factors pointed to an accidental death but did not logically preclude homicide. Was Charlie capable of murdering his own father and making it look like an accident? He would have been about sixteen years old at the time. He had no criminal record of any kind. Juvenile records, if he had any, were sealed, but could be accessed by law enforcement if there was sufficient cause. Dave could investigate that possibility with his Pasco contacts.

Maybe there was another way to approach the problem of getting Charlie to show his hand. Paz had said that he saw a diamond engagement ring in Charlie's vehicle during the traffic stop he'd made. Possible that a call to Charlie's mother on that matter might shake something loose. Dave might be a good choice to do something like that since he'd already established a relationship of sorts with Charlie's mother. On the other hand, Paz had actually seen the ring and could call to verify ownership plausibly. Maybe.

Paz agreed to use his best interviewing skills to contact Mrs. Crane from the Keys "just to make sure" she knew the whereabouts of something so valuable. It was not standard operating procedure to make such a call, but neither was there anything wrong with doing so. It could be framed as positive police engagement with the community, if the "community" could be framed as including most of the state of Florida.

Mrs. Crane answered the telephone and confided in Paz that "quite a few police officers have been checking up on my welfare. It's nice. They haven't done that in a long time."

She readily confirmed that "Charlie has a girl," and that she'd voluntarily given her son her diamond engagement ring for the girl.

"It is quite small, but of decent quality, I believe. I have no sentimental attachment to it of any kind."

Did Mrs. Crane know the fiancée?

"No, but I hear she may be moving in with us soon. If I can believe what my son says."

Paz thanked Mrs. Crane and reported the conversation to Joel.

"She'll tell her son about the call and the conversation," Joel said. "We need to be ready for his reaction."

Next, Joel called Dave once more, his law enforcement contact up in Pasco County, to see what he could find out about the Crane family's history in the neighborhood.

Dave was well-known in Dade City and had a good reputation. He didn't live in the Cranes' immediate area but told Joel he was open to informally talking with some of the people who did live near them.

The Cranes had moved to the Victorian about forty years earlier from Pennsylvania, up near Pittsburgh. Charlie had been a very young child when they came, an only child with no close friends.

Household after household reported fairly consistently that the Cranes had kept to themselves but were pleasant enough in public. Charlie was a smart little kid who did well in school but was not particularly well-liked. He tended to associate with younger children in elementary school, but he bullied them a bit. He was dependable with his paper route. He didn't function well in groups, like the Cub Scouts. He enjoyed talking about short-wave radios and brought in simple electronic projects he'd made at home to show off. Some of the teachers that

Dave could reach remembered him because he was an excellent student who daydreamed quite a bit in class. Not uncommon with bright kids.

It wasn't until he finally was able to speak with the neighbor whose property adjoined the Cranes' yard at the back fence that Dave learned anything specifically concerning. Mrs. Trautman was close to eighty and had occupied her home behind the Crane property for over fifty years, before the Cranes had arrived from Pennsylvania. Or was it Ohio?

She was a little hard of hearing and tended to talk loudly. Dave looked back at the Cranes' house over the fence and steered her toward the far side of her property.

She had a lot to say.

"Nobody would let that boy anywhere near their animals. He was always back there near the fence digging little graves and putting up markers, like a cemetery. He trapped squirrels, and that would be that. People started watching their little dogs after a while. Because, otherwise, they might disappear.

"We knew that boy was doing things, maybe awful things, or at least had something to do with the missing pets, but you couldn't say a word to his parents.

"His mother would deny it, and maybe cry and shut the door, and nobody would say 'boo' to the father. He was not sociable. He would just turn his back and walk off if anyone said anything that he didn't like. He died in his garage when the boy was still fairly young. Some of us went to the funeral, but none of us felt very bad about him being gone.

"The boy grew up and went away to college for a while, but then he came back. Lived with his mother ever since. He does quite a bit of work on the yard - it's a nice one. Does a nice job. Never been inside the house."

Joel knew this background information about Charlie's family was concerning. Childhood cruelty to animals often means abuse is going on in the family behind closed doors, and young animal abusers may grow up to be sociopaths or, at least, lack empathy for others' feelings.

Chapter 27
No Magic Like That Exists

    Catherine dressed for work, gave Rocky a goodbye pat, made sure her side of the duplex was locked, and drove to the Sparkling Tarpon.

    The Sunday afternoon crowd was jovial and starting to get loud. Several tables, mostly couples, were drinking margaritas or pitchers of beer and eating Florida Keys appetizer specialties. Catherine smiled at them, almost a job requirement, and soon was in better spirits.

    It doesn't have to be such a big drama, she told herself as she went from table to table taking orders and bringing food and drink. I kissed a hot guy that I slept with twenty years ago. I'm glad I got to find out what happened to him, what his life path has been. That's all it was, and that's okay.

    We're older, and we've both been through a lot since Mexico. Our paths diverged, and then crossed again in this crazy way. If it weren't for Charlie, we would probably have never seen each other again...unless he stopped me for speeding or something as random as that, she joked to herself.

But her heart wasn't so sure it was that simple and clear-cut. Her longing surprised her. Was she perhaps mourning a road she hadn't taken in her youth? Was she reaching back to a time when she didn't yet know the grief of losing a husband? Was she imagining that a re-do with Joel would somehow wipe away all the residuals of grief and some of the regrets about her choices over the decades? No magic like that exists. The magic in her life here and now was in the aqua blue of the ocean sparkling in the sun and in the softly stirring tropical breezes and in the fragrance of tropical flowers at night in the humid air.

***

Joel prepared himself to leave home for his three twelve-hour shifts in Monroe County. He would take the cooler of food that Carmela had made for him, and his clothes and his grooming items, and arrive at the bachelor apartment, as Carmella had started to call it, before nine o'clock. The tropical sky would have just gone dark. The highway traffic would be heavy heading north with weekend visitors leaving the Keys, but they wouldn't be his problem tonight. He wasn't on duty yet, and he would be heading south.

When is it too late to take a chance on your heart's desire? The thought surfaced unbidden. Joel tried to shake it off. Was Catherine his heart's desire? He couldn't bear to hurt Carmela, and nor did he intend to. He didn't want to break anyone's heart. Maybe there would be no emotional damage if he just took it slow and focused on his main objective: protecting Catherine from danger in the form of Charlie Crane. Assuming Catherine was right about the identity of the guy who had been stalking her. Or, who she believed had been stalking her. She could be wrong.

Chapter 28
A Bridal Suite

Charlie was still a little agitated. He'd been on edge ever since his mother had said terrible things to him, implying that Catherine was a figment of his imagination. She'd actually used the word 'figment.' Catherine was not imaginary. She was real. Why would his own mother want to think that he could never get a girl?

He felt quite suddenly that he needed to go see Catherine again. Right now. Everything was taken care of up here in Dade City, he reasoned. It was late, but if he got tired, he would just pull over in a rest area.

He threw a few important items into a nap sack, took a garment bag from his closet, and went to his mother's room to tell her he was leaving again for just a few days.

She was sitting up in bed reading when Charlie came into her bedroom. It wasn't a Victorian-style room, it was actually Victorian. It had green Victorian wallpaper, well over a hundred years old, a leafy design of entangled stems and florets. For a while in the Nineteenth Century, copper arsenite had been widely used to create the vivid greens used in some of the era's wallpapers. Charlie wondered if there were still traces of arsenic behind the paper on their walls.

"Mother," he said quietly. "I'm going to go back to the Florida Keys tonight to see if I can bring Catherine home with me. Do you think you'll be OK for another few days if I go tonight?"

She looked ready to fall asleep. Pretty drowsy.

"I already took my medications," she said.

"Do you want to see the room I fixed up for me and Catherine upstairs?"

"I don't think so, not tonight. I'm too tired to go up those stairs."

"OK, then. I'll just get your coffee ready for you for the morning before I leave. There's lots of food here."

"I only eat cereal with a half of a banana in the morning."

"That's fine, Mother. I'm going to get going now. Goodbye. I love you."

"I know you do, dear. I won't tell that policeman anything if he comes back. What should I say?"

"Just say I'm not here. You don't have to give anyone any details, you know. Just be nice and relaxed."

"What if he won't take 'no' for an answer?"

"If he wants to talk to me, he'll have to come back. Because I won't be here. Simple as that."

There was a slight chill in the air. Charlie had decided to take some camping supplies, this time. He'd put some foam rubber in the trunk, and a sleeping bag as well. It might come in handy. His supplies were all in order and loaded. He'd be back at the Lobster Hut Motel in time to catch a nice morning nap. It felt good to be back on the road headed south.

Before he left, he had prepared two special rooms, one upstairs, and one downstairs. The upstairs room wasn't his old childhood bedroom that he still used as his own. It was, instead, a large bedroom on the third floor with tall windows on two sides, hardwood floors and nice oak furniture. He had made up the bed with white and cream sheets and blankets, and had ordered plush, expensive pillows stuffed with Hungarian goose down. He had added some touches of silver with the accessories, including an antique silver hand mirror and hairbrush. It was a bridal suite.

The other room was a lot more basic. A single bed. A small chest. A toilet and sink. Florescent lights. Blackout shades on the two high, small windows that looked out into window wells. Not exactly the basement, but, well.... the basement. And a door that locked. From the outside. With a padlock.

He hoped it wouldn't come to that, but it was always better to be prepared.

Chapter 29
Second Thoughts

It was Carmela who called Emil. It was Friday evening.

"What's going on, *viejo amigo*?"

He came over, and this time it was different. She wasn't playing coy. She had something of the lost little girl in her eyes. There was a vulnerability about her and, if he was honest, it was a little sad.

Who was he to turn a woman down, especially a woman who was as crazy about him as Carmella was?

She'd probably never completely gotten over him, Emil reasoned. Now, Joel was away a little more than she could handle.

He thought about it for a while, as she snuggled up against him on the couch. She was warm and pliable.

It wasn't like it hadn't happened before. And it wasn't his own marriage vows that he would be breaking. Jamie had left him. Who knows if they'd ever get back together? Joel's marriage is just not my problem right now, Emil thought.

If Joel found out...Carmela would maybe get this house and Joel would keep his pension when he retired. Joel could get ice cold when he was angry. He would probably walk out, get a tough lawyer, and wash his hands of them both.

Carmela would expect him, Emil, to fill in all the gaps in her life after Joel was gone.

Did he even want Carmela, full-time? A sad, guilty Carmella? He definitely preferred a fun, flirty Carmella, the girl who had always been nuts about him.

Joel must not be giving her what she needed. Did *he* have something on the side? Saint Joel?

Emil shrugged, and kissed Carmela like he hadn't kissed her in more than a decade and a half. His hands and his mouth knew where to go. It was territory he had completely explored before, a long time ago to be sure, but he knew where to touch, just so, and where to kiss. She closed her eyes, shaking her head 'no,' as his fingers and lips found every little place.

But he stopped. He smelled the alcohol on her breath. Did he really need this in his life right now?

"What's the matter?" she asked.

"I don't think this is the right time," Emil answered, sitting up. "I want you to really, really think about it. You cross this line, and there won't be any going back."

Carmella sat up, arranging her clothing. "Since when did you get impulse control?" She sounded a little wounded. She had put her marriage vows on the table before him, and he'd passed.

"I know a few more things than I knew when we were young. We can wait for a better time. You need to think about all the possible consequences, *Chica*."

Carmela felt worse than she had in a long time. Shamed by Emil Martin, whom she'd never imagined had any shame at all where women were concerned.

***

Charlie drove down Highway 27 in the starless night and began to have some second thoughts. He really wasn't taking Catherine's needs and feelings into consideration. It is important to do things right if you want a good start to a marriage.

She would probably want to wear a beautiful wedding dress.

He pulled over and used his smart phone to find what he needed. There was just the place in Key Largo. It didn't open until 9:30 in the morning, so he would maybe pull into John Pennekamp Coral Reef State Park and snooze for a while once he got to the Keys.

The used clothing store was late opening, fifteen minutes late to be exact. Charlie found three wedding dresses and selected one that he thought would fit Catherine best. It was all fluffy white lace and satin ribbons, machine-made certainly, but what could you expect in a Size 8 for thirty-five dollars?

He had the ring, the dress, and the veil.

He knew it wouldn't be a legitimate marriage unless it was registered with the state.

However, he had become more accepting of entering into some kind of an extra-legitimate union with Catherine. A private ceremony. He'd been thinking so much about what her naked body would look like that he felt he couldn't wait for her to come around to the idea of marriage on her own timetable. He had to have her. He spent part of almost every day reading about all the things he could do to that body in their marriage bed, and he was eager to try a lot of them. He wanted to take her full breasts in his hands and squeeze them and stuff them in his mouth. He wanted to hear her scream with pleasure and beg him for more, the way the girls did in the books and on the videos when they were tied up and sucked and pinched and mounted from behind.

No one would be likely to perform a legal marriage ceremony if she arrived at a wedding chapel chloroformed, much less at a city hall if she were in that condition.

They would have to first be married in their hearts, he decided, and then they could eventually make it legal in Pasco County once she was ready for that step. If he got her pregnant right away, it might speed along her decision-making process. It had with his mother, Charlie had always suspected. He would just keep having her, over and over, up in their third-floor suite until her belly was full with his child.

It wouldn't take too long. She'd be pregnant within a month. She would never leave then. She'd have to stay, like his mother did. Would their first baby be a boy or a girl?

Chapter 30
Joel Makes the Paper

A pile-up southbound before the Seven Mile Bridge had traffic backed up all the way past Marathon to Duck Key. Joel, with his lights flashing, threaded his way through the lanes of stubborn drivers who refused to give way, to the detriment of everyone on the road that morning.

An ambivalently suicidal man in his forties was the proximate cause of the traffic jam. On a sunny, bright Saturday, he stood on the outside of the concrete bridge rail, holding on with both hands, looking back over his shoulder at the water. He seemed to be contemplating pushing off with his feet and dropping backward into the ocean thirty feet below.

"Don't try to stop me!" he yelled at Joel and his partner.

"Wasn't going to," Joel replied. He stepped back, resting casually against the rail, a few feet from the man. "I came out this morning to talk to you. Where are your kids?"

"Wife's got them. I'm never going to see them again, she said."

"For sure, if you jump," Joel replied calmly. "Divorced?"

"Not yet. She's got a boyfriend."

"Who's going to raise your kids if you're gone?"

"She says I'm a drunk and I don't deserve to see them."

"Have you had something to drink this morning?"

"What do you think?"

"You know, people can go a different route. They can get sober. It's not easy, but it's not rocket science. There are people who want to help you."

"Why do you care?"

"Well, partly because after you die, your kids and everyone else will always blame themselves for what happened. Did I make Daddy die? Is it my fault that he didn't want to be with me anymore? It just leaves a trail of pain through the years. No one wants that for their kids. People get sober. Problems get fixed."

"You have any family problems?"

Joel shrugged. "I've definitely got some big ones. But I'm not hanging over the wrong side of a bridge this morning. Can I give you a hand up?"

"It's embarrassing. Everyone is looking at me."

"They're hoping you'll come back up so they can get going down to Key West and start their weekend."

Joel glanced at his partner. "I'm going to help you climb back over to this side, and we'll take it from there. One step at a time."

***

The front page of the *Key West City News* weekend edition ran a color photo of Joel standing on the bridge against the backdrop of the blue ocean and the miles-long line of traffic. Charlie skimmed the story as he ate breakfast back at the Lobster Hut. His room had been undisturbed when he'd gotten in earlier. All seemed to be going as planned.

He'd ordered some fresh sliced avocado with his scrambled eggs and toast. He was going to need to sleep for a while, so he'd asked the bartender to mix him a strong screwdriver. The bartender hadn't blinked. This was a routine request at seven in the morning in the Florida Keys. Mimosas on Sunday, and screwdrivers or a Bloody Mary the rest of the week.

When he'd finished reading the story, Charlie studied the photograph of Joel on the bridge. Monroe County Sheriff's Deputy Joel Miller looked a little familiar.

Catherine. The blond cop that knew Catherine. Charlie had seen him come out of her side of the duplex. Why was he there? Charlie tried to remember what the guy had been wearing that morning. He had been out of uniform.

Was he someone she knew? Could it have been her plan all along to move down to the Keys from Tampa to be with the cop? Had he made love to her? If he'd had her, if he'd done any of those things that Charlie wanted to do...Charlie shook off the images. He was ready, absolutely ready this time, to take Catherine for himself. Question is, how do you kill a cop? Charlie considered some of the approaches that he could take, painful ones and more practical ones.

He would look in on Catherine later. Maybe they would talk. Maybe she would come home with him.

Chapter 31
Carmela and Emil

Carmela called Emil again on Saturday morning and asked him to come over to look at the pool pump. It was sending out a stream of fine bubbles, rather than a forceful flow of water. He told her to shut off the pump and that he'd be by when he had a chance.

Nothing is going to happen, she told herself in the shower. She blow-dried her curls with the diffuser attachment and put on the makeup she'd normally wear for work.

She reached into her drawer and found herself holding her sexiest underwear. She put on a pair of loose-fitting white shorts and an orange tank top. Gold earrings, a gold bracelet, and white wedge sandals completed what she knew was a pretty hot tropical look.

Too bad Joel wasn't around to appreciate it. And when he was around, he was always thinking about work.

Carmela examined her face in the mirror. She definitely had a few age spots, and her chin line wasn't tight anymore. She knew women who had Botox and filler injections as casually as they used a curling iron. That might be next for me, she thought, although I don't want to look like some of those girls. I just wish I looked more like I did when I was younger.

Her figure was still pretty good. She had nice legs. They weren't short, even though she was only 5'3". I need to get back to the gym, she thought, turning her head to inspect how she looked from behind.

Emil arrived and turned the pool pump back on. They could hear it catch, and then it began to suck pool water normally. He checked the pool strainers.

"You need to empty these every day, Chica. You know that, don't you?"

She shrugged. "I forgot. I'm sorry you came all the way over here for nothing...would you like something to drink?"

Emil sighed. It was nine o'clock in the morning. "Vodka and grapefruit juice?"

"No grapefruit. Orange?"

Emil nodded. Did he really want this to happen again? Her ass looked pretty hot in those shorts.

Jamie had had him served with papers this morning. He'd opened the door to get the newspaper, and boom. Just like that. Another divorce. The last he'd heard, she was due to have a baby any week now, Dennis' baby. She was long gone.

Emil set his drink down and followed Carmella into the kitchen. She was standing at the island. He pushed up against her from behind. She stopped what she was doing, but she didn't turn around, and she didn't say 'no.' He slid his hands up and took both her breasts and squeezed gently. He heard her breath catch. He lowered his face to her hair and kissed her neck. He pulled down her shorts, turned her around, and lifted her up onto the granite countertop. He slipped his finger inside her. Definitely ready for him. Just like how things were in the old days, he thought, before life got so complicated and so ...disappointing.

Chapter 32
Joel and Catherine and Charlie

His shift was over, and he could have gone back to the cottage he was renting, or even all the way home, up to Kendall. Maybe he should have. Instead, he headed south and pulled into Catherine's driveway just before the sun went down.

He sat for a few minutes, considering how people make the choices they end up making. If I, as a law enforcement officer, squeeze the trigger to shoot someone who is attacking either me or someone I'm sworn to protect, is that the moment of choice? Or was it when I first arrived at the scene and started thinking about what I might need to do? When I got up that morning and went to work, knowing anything could happen that day? When I decided to apply to become a police officer? When I was trained in firearms and marksmanship in the military? How about back when I was a little kid and gleefully shot my brother in the face with a squirt gun?

Joel reviewed, not for the first time, the choice he had made more than twenty years ago the morning he'd gotten into the taxi waiting for him along the quay in Cozumel, leaving Catherine standing there. He hadn't turned back to wave to her as the taxi pulled away. He hadn't asked for her address. He'd thought it would be less traumatic for them both to just rip the bandage off and make it a knife-clean break.

Now, he was going to make a different choice. He left Carmella a message saying that he wouldn't be back home tonight and walked up to Catherine's door.

"I saw you sitting there. I wasn't sure if you were going to come in."

He replied simply, "I need to take a quick shower."

"Tough day?"

"About average."

He got out of the shower, and still naked, took her hand and led her to the bedroom. She could see the scars on his bare flesh. The past wounds. The near misses.

They had more skills than when they were young and in Mexico but chose to first retrace familiar ground with their kisses and caresses. They could feel each other's hearts pounding as their bodies pressed together.

She still knew his scent and the feel of his kisses. She nipped his neck lightly, leaving no mark, and left a trail of kisses down to his navel and tasted his flesh.

Afterwards, they clung to each other in her bed and fell asleep in each other's arms. Rocky sat up on Catherine's dresser, looking out the window. The sheer white curtains were open and lifted and billowed as the breeze came up. Rocky froze, and then jumped down and slunk under the bed.

Charlie thought he was going to die. He literally could not take a breath. His heart seemed to have stopped, and then it started racing so fast that he felt it might rupture in his chest. Blood rushed to his face, and then drained away so completely that he thought he would faint and fall to the ground outside her window. He must have made a sound because the cat jumped down and left.

At the sun's first light, Charlie watched the guy come out of Catherine's place shirtless, carrying a cup of coffee. He stretched his strong-looking, lithe body and circled his head, getting the crunches out of his neck.

Catherine followed him out moments later, wearing a short beach robe. They leaned up against the patrol car, kissing. The cop put his hands on Catherine's bare bottom and pulled her tight up against his hips. She whispered something in his ear, and they both went back inside the house.

Charlie waited. It was unbearable, so he started to count off the seconds. He was all the way up to two thousand and six before the cop came out again. Catherine wasn't with him. His face looked relaxed, and his stride was loose and confident.

Charlie thought he would get into his patrol car and drive away, but he stopped. He began to scan carefully around the neighborhood. His eyes rested on the place where Charlie was concealed in the shadows, and it seemed like he might take a step in that direction. But his cell phone buzzed, and he returned to his patrol car and took off.

Charlie's mood had sunk so low that it was as if he were buried in quicksand. He couldn't make it to his car, which was parked far down the street. He might have to crawl on his hands and knees across the sharp crushed limestone pebbles to get there. Despair. Black despair. If he didn't fight it off, he could remain immobile for hours.

Before he had met Catherine, he sometimes had to lie on the floor of his bedroom all day long, so black was his mood, so incapacitating was his emotional agony.

He did not deserve to be treated so callously. He wanted to choke the swagger right out of that cop. He wanted to pound himself into Catherine until he was drained, and then he wanted to choke the life out of her, too. As his anger boiled up, it gave him the energy to get to his feet and walk to his car. The soulless whore would be trussed up in his trunk and halfway to Dade City before that cop ever had the chance to come back for more.

Chapter 33
Might As Well Be Real About What We're Doing

Charlie watched Catherine leave for work. The neighborhood was quiet. He slipped around the duplex to the ocean side and jimmied open the sliding glass door. The living room was neat, but in the bedroom, the sheets were tangled, and the pillows were on the floor. It smelled like sex.

Charlie wanted to sit down and cry. Catherine. His almost-fiancée' and the mother-to-be of his son. The evidence of her infidelity was draining his life force. He could barely tolerate being in the room where she had been with that cop, but he had no choice but to finish what he'd started.

He found a suitcase in her closet, and systematically sifted through her clothing and lingerie, selecting only things that he wanted to see her wearing. He scooped up some of her grooming items, and then carried the packed suitcase down the street to his car.

He got what he needed from the vehicle, arranged the trunk, and went back inside the duplex to wait for Catherine to come home again.

He sat quietly, reviewing his plan. Eventually, Rocky came out from wherever he had been hiding and strolled over to Charlie. He remembers me, Charlie thought. His mood began to lighten.

What to do, what to do about Catherine's cat? There were only three options that Charlie could see, given his timetable. They could bring Rocky to Dade City with them. He could turn the cat loose outside to fend for itself. Or he could kill it and be done with it.

Killing the cat would be easy, but it would surely turn Catherine against him. Besides, he rather liked Rocky. A cat is a perfectly capable hunter in his own right. Turning him loose outside in the neighborhood here would give the cat the opportunity to survive on his own terms. He decided he would only kill the cat, or threaten to kill it, if Catherine put up resistance to coming home to Dade City with him.

***

Carmella had spent the morning cleaning and doing laundry. She'd watered the potted plants on the patio and around the pool, prepared some food, and was now wondering if Joel was going to be coming home from the Keys later on. She almost hoped that, today, he wouldn't.

Things were different in her mind since it seemed that Emil was getting divorced. She felt like she had a choice. She could stay with Joel or go with Emil.

It broke her heart to think of hurting Joel.

He wasn't a man to discuss his feelings much, even when they were younger, before he was a cop. He would listen, and think about things, and then make some pinpoint accurate observation. Now, after all the years as a cop, he was probably even less likely to be lighthearted about situations, but just as likely to be straightforward.

She knew he wouldn't hit her, but it was very possible that he would punch out Emil's lights.

She should warn Emil when he came over.

"I don't think you should tell him," Emil said. "We don't have any kind of a plan. We really haven't thought about this."

"I've been thinking about it. I've been thinking about it since we were in high school. I broke my marriage vows for you."

Emil sighed. "I just don't know, Carmella. We should wait."

"I've been waiting since high school."

"Do you really want this now, as a grown woman, or are you still thinking with the mind-set and the heart of a sixteen-year-old? Because we aren't sixteen. There are real consequences. People are going to get hurt. And we won't get away scot-free. There's going to be a price to pay."

"You always get so cautious and sensible when it comes time to get real about us. How come you never say 'no' when your dick is hard?"

Emil sighed again. "Truthfully? Because there's usually alcohol involved. I probably wouldn't have done half the things I've done in my life, sober."

"Now you're claiming a drinking problem? That's why you did what you did with me?"

"I don't mean that. I just mean that it's hard for me to do the right thing sometimes when I've had a few. It's harder to resist temptation."

"I think you mean it's easier to do what you want to do. It is, for me."

"This really isn't a good time for me. I'm not thinking straight. I guess I'm messed up from the divorce."

"Which you caused by your own behavior."

"You may be right, but it feels like, all of a sudden, you're pressuring me. Can we take it slow? See how things go for a while?"

Carmela wiped her tears away. "Make me a drink?"

Emil looked at the bottle. He poured them both a vodka on the rocks with no juice mixer. Might as well be real about what we're doing here, he thought. We aren't drinking it for the Vitamin C.

Chapter 34
I'm Nothing If Not Flexible

Charlie sat on Catherine's couch with Rocky on his lap. He had the chloroform and the rags ready. He'd read up on the various EPA warnings and had what he thought would be a reasonably safe and effective plan. Overpower her. Knock her out with not too much chloroform. Quickly go get the car and back it up to the front door. Put her in the trunk. Stop some place to tie her up and gag her for when she came to. Drive off the Keys.

Getting her in to the trunk without hurting her could be a little tricky. Even though she was slender, she was tall, so she no doubt weighed enough to make it difficult. He would probably have to pull her by her armpits, legs dragging, to the open trunk, and then get her in as best he could without bruising her too much.

Leave the door open for the cat to make up his own mind about where he wanted to go, and we're on our way to our new life together.

Charlie reviewed the plan one more time. Everything was ready to go.

He relaxed on Catherine's couch, waiting for her. Soon, he heard the crunch of tires on the gravel driveway. He got up and peeked out the kitchen window. A white stretch limo was parked at the other side of the duplex. A girl said something to the driver, and he wheeled the limo out toward the Overseas Highway. The girl stood out front, looking the place over, and then unlocked the entrance door on the other side of the duplex and went in.

After a few minutes, she came back out with a stepladder. He watched her set up and attach some kind of electronic device to the fascia board, climb down the ladder, and go out back to the ocean side.

Charlie took the opportunity to pick up the chloroform and rags and quickly exit the front door. He made it to his car and drove off without having to pass the duplex again on his way out of the neighborhood and back to the Overseas Highway.

Complications, Charlie thought. Not what I need now at this point. There are some other parts of the plan, though, some other steps that I can take. There's a gun range up in Pasco that's going to be getting my business. I'm nothing if not flexible.

Charlie stopped by his motel to gather up some of his belongings, paid for some more days, and was off the Keys and on the 18 Mile Stretch heading toward Florida City before Catherine even returned home.

***

The first thing Catherine noticed was that Kate was back in town, up on a ladder, and doing something with a cordless drill.

"Good to see you! Let's catch up when you're done!"

Catherine went inside and greeted Rocky, who was meowing and pacing restlessly.

"I missed you, too, Sweetie! How about a delicious fish and shrimp dinner?"

After she fed the cat, she went to her bedroom to change clothes, a glass of white wine with ice in her hand. The room seemed disturbed. Had she left her black negligee out on the bed? Definitely not. She hadn't worn it, well, not at all since she'd moved down from Tampa. In the bathroom, her toothpaste, most of her grooming supplies, and her makeup bag were gone.

Without hesitating, she called Joel's cell number, and he called her back right away.

"I can't come now, but you should make a report. I'm going to ask Paz to come by as soon as he can. And I don't think you should stay there."

"Kate is back. Maybe I could stay next door with her..."

"You should probably both leave until things get settled." Joel paused. "The two of you are welcome to stay at the cottage I rent on Plantation Key. I'll be up in the Miami area for a couple of days, so the place will be all yours."

"I don't know if Kate will go for it, but she might. Her parents would certainly want her to."

***

Back home in Dade City, Charlie found everything was just fine with his mother. Pretty much. Just the usual complaints.

"We're out of milk. No one called, except you. No one came to the door. We got only junk mail. I've been here all alone."

"I can go up to the convenience store to get milk."

She shrugged. "You've had a long drive. It can wait until morning."

"I suppose you're wondering where Catherine is."

"Catherine? Who's she?"

"Never mind. We'll talk about it later. Good night, Mother."

The next morning after breakfast, Charlie headed to the *Dade City Aces Shooting Range and Gun Club* with his new-ish Taurus G2C 9mm pistol for some practice. He'd bought it a while ago with his mother's credit card back when he'd found out that Catherine had moved out of her house in Tampa without telling him.

Originally, he had been so distraught that his plan had been to use it on himself. Then, once he'd calmed down and had traced Catherine to the Keys–her friend Tanya at her old job had been more helpful with that than she'd perhaps realized-- he was thinking of maybe just killing her, and then himself. Romeo and Juliet. He'd dismissed that idea in favor of taking her alive, bringing her back home, and making her his bride, his concubine, his prisoner–her choice. Now, he was thinking more like kill the cop, take Catherine, and live happily ever after. He still had to iron out the details.

He assumed the cop was good with firearms. But he was also sure the cop wasn't as smart as he, Charlie, was. Anyone can learn to be a cop, he thought. Not everyone had Charlie's brains. Fewer than two percent of the population did, to put a more precise number on it. Charlie was quite sure he could have Catherine stuffed into his trunk and out of the Keys and into his cellar for a mandatory training and disciplinary period before the cop even woke up to the fact that she was gone. The details of the plan varied, depending on the mood Charlie was in.

But one thing was for sure: he would be at the shooting range as soon as it opened whenever he was in town. Practice makes perfect, as his mother had always said. And he'd been practicing in his own way ever since he'd been a kid, so he'd certainly found that saying to be true.

Chapter 35
How Did He Even Find You?

Catherine arrived with Kate and Rocky at Joel's cottage after she had finished her short dinner shift at the Sparkling Tarpon. Kate had come along to the restaurant and kept watch on Rocky in his cat carrier while Catherine served drinks and fish sandwiches.

Kate was initially not too thrilled to leave the duplex, because she had intended to set up the new monitoring equipment she'd brought down with her from her parents' home and give it a thorough test run. Catherine convinced her that she could maybe work on some of it in Islamorada.

"Want to hear what happened while you were away?" Catherine asked.

"Sure. But I think I already know most of it. My parents got the various police reports. They were, like, totally beside themselves. You have no idea what I had to go through to get back down here. We'll be the first ones to hear anything if either one of those two guys from Key West makes bail or gets cut loose with reduced charges."

The sun had almost set. Kate and Catherine took a bottle of cold wine and some sliced cheese and Italian bread out to the dock. The water and the sky were both a grayish-purple, and the surface of the ocean was as flat as an oil slick. The horizon was barely distinguishable.

"It would be a nice evening to take out these kayaks," Kate said as she flicked on the dock lights.

Catherine looked around. "I don't think so."

"Right, right. You were almost kidnapped. Here." Kate poured her some more wine. "Chill out. How did he even find you?"

Catherine shrugged. "I think Tanya, a woman I worked with up in Tampa, must have told him. I'd invited her to come down, so she knew where I lived."

"Nice friend."

"She didn't know. Charlie seems pretty normal on the surface." Catherine paused. "I didn't even know, not really. And when weird stuff started happening down here after a while, I really thought it could have been those guys who were after you. It seemed way more probable."

Kate nodded. "Stupid thing is, stupid on their part, is that I never even saw what they thought I saw, that murder. I guess I've gotten so dependent on my electronic surveillance goodies that I don't pay enough attention to my own eyes and ears. Not to make you paranoid more than you are, but I wonder if he could find us here..."

"I don't know if he's still around, or where he stays." Catherine paused, thinking. "You know, even though I was glad we called the sheriff when I first saw that dead bird at our duplex that night, I wasn't really, truly convinced it was him. Not at first. If you hadn't pushed it, I might have just let it go. I just couldn't believe that he'd find me all the way down in the Keys, or even want to find me. Honestly, we never really had much of a relationship at all."

"Could he find you where we are now, at this place?"

"I don't think so. Only if he followed us. So—I doubt it." Catherine shivered. "So creepy that he took my clothes and things."

Kate said, "You know what I think, don't you?"

Catherine shook her head.

"That stuff that he took out of your apartment...your clothes and toothpaste and all that? Those things were supposed to be your supplies, like your necessities for a trip. I bet he was about to come back in a few minutes with his car and get you, next."

Chapter 36
Down Time

Carmella was sitting out by the pool when Joel got home from the Keys.

The drive on this evening hadn't been so long as it was stressful. Keys traffic in the season tended to be an annoying mix of impatient drivers, drunk drivers, and tourists distracted by the scenery. Pedestrians and bicyclists, mostly people on vacation, were inclined to ignore traffic signals and niceties like using the crosswalks. Once he was off the Keys, Joel usually took Krome Avenue, depending on the time of day, to avoid Miami-area interstate traffic.

He sat down beside Carmella on a poolside lounge chair to decompress.

"Can I get you something to drink?"

"That would be nice."

She came back with a cold beer for each of them.

"What do you want to do on your days off?"

Joel shrugged. He hadn't really thought about it. "Maybe something outdoors. We could go out fishing with your cousin and the kids."

People who work in law enforcement can find that the job eventually takes over their identity if they don't make a conscious, consistent effort to plan "normal" recreation with "normal" people. The dangerous and unpredictable elements of the job can gradually create a threat-based view of the world. The alert, vigilant, energized cop on duty comes home and crashes. The adrenaline of the street, the constant hyper-awareness, the necessity of assessing every single person and every single situation, dissipates at home, leaving somebody who is tired to the core and who might want to be alone for a good while. The roller coaster highs of the job swinging to the lows of off-time can lead to destructive spending, gambling, and deteriorated family relationships.

Joel ran, worked out at the gym, and liked to get out on the water when he could. Sometimes that worked. Sometimes, it didn't.

The *Bluewater 355e* motored past Fisher Island and headed south toward Key Biscayne. Carmella played "I spy" with her cousin's two kids. The older boy was a good sport about it; the six-year-old excitedly pointed to the various aids to navigation, and to the colorful boats of the Coconut Grove Kids' Sailing Regatta twirling about just offshore.

The day was perfect. Light ocean swells, a mostly blue sky, and just enough of an offshore breeze kept everyone cool and comfortable as the boat toured the islands off the coast of

Greater Miami. Carmella was in an outgoing, buoyant mood that made the outing fun for everyone.

Joel taught the kids to fish for snook. They enjoyed the picnic that Carmella and her cousin's wife had put together for the family. In the afternoon, they put the boat ashore at Virginia Key, and the kids ran around the beach until it was time to motor back.

After the boat was tied up at the marina, Joel taught the kids how to properly hose it down, and they all headed to Steve's Dockside Grill for a light dinner. The kids bickered about menu options. Joel's thoughts started to turn to Catherine and her safety.

"You did good today," Carmella said to him, "but I can see you're starting to think about your job, something at work again."

Joel looked into her dark brown eyes and felt discomfort about his lies of omission.

Carmela had been a good partner for him, and he knew he was lucky. Life with a cop is never a bowl of cherries. For years, she'd had to wonder how his mood would be after each work shift out there on the streets. Would he come home alive, or would she get that call? There were the periods when he'd been assigned to Internal Affairs that he'd worried about potential threats to her safety – from *inside* the organization. He'd always felt that their decision not to have kids was a good one, but when he watched her play with her cousin's children, he felt that maybe she had been cheated of something she would have been good at and enjoyed.

Nothing could keep him from doing his job of protecting Catherine, but it unsettled him that they had crossed a line. Catherine did not deserve to be cast as "the other woman" in his domestic drama. Joel had never thought of himself as a man cut out for the starring role of "two-timing husband." Every little lie he would have to tell Carmela, every part of himself that he would have to keep separate from both women, would in some way damage the relationships, bit by bit. He'd never been like that. Many other men...and women...he knew seemed to manage it almost casually. But not "Saint Joel," as his brother Emil sometimes mockingly called him.

But whatever his beliefs were about himself, whatever his self-professed values, he had gone ahead with Catherine without putting on the brakes. It surprised him that, when he was spending the night with her, he hadn't given a thought to his other life. They'd been together down in Mexico when they were both very young. They had been lovers before he'd ever dated Carmela. Before he'd spent one day in the Army. Before he'd known for sure that he was going to have a career in law enforcement. Being with Catherine now felt like stepping back into that before-time when he was less tarnished by life. It seemed natural. It felt right, even though he couldn't morally justify it.

They had a magnetic attraction to each other. But even magnets can be kept apart. Could he manage that?

***

Catherine didn't know Joel's wife. He had barely talked about her. Catherine didn't know her age. Her hair color.

What model car she drove. All she knew was that they didn't have kids, they lived together in Kendall, and she'd worked in real estate sales.

Catherine imagined a petite brunette with an outgoing, confident personality. She was a woman very different from herself, but the one that Joel had chosen to marry.

Catherine was now "the other woman" in this soap opera. It was a part she did not want. Letting Joel go again after two decades apart was something she believed she would be theoretically able to do, because she had lived most of her adult life without him.

But, after the night they'd spent together, after her passion for him had been re-ignited, after the way her body hummed and felt alive again, she didn't see herself being the one to put an end to it.

Chapter 37
A Visit with Charlie's Mother

Pasco County Deputy David Raspin found himself with a little time and decided to try to help his old Army buddy, Joel Miller, by checking out a few things about the Crane boy.

With a little luck and some help from a couple of old timers in the department, he was able to dig up the lead investigator's notes from almost thirty years ago. The father's death seemed to have been pretty well reviewed by the insurance company as well as by the Sheriff's Criminal Investigations Department.

What was of more interest to Raspin was a death in the immediate neighborhood just a few months earlier that had also been filed as accidental. However, it bore certain parallels to the Crane death: an older man had died unattended in his home from a head injury stemming from a fall. Each body was discovered within a day or less, and the medical examiner cleared them both as accidental.

What are the odds?

Pretty good, as it turns out. Traumatic brain injury from falls resulting in death occurs over 17,000 times a year. Most of the dead are older adults.

Raspin asked around the neighborhood, but no one was still alive who might have remembered anything pertinent.

Raspin decided to go on another fishing trip and drove over to the Crane residence.

Mrs. Crane seemed lucid and invited him in for a glass of iced tea. Charlie's vehicle was not in the driveway.

"I don't know where he is. He went out this morning. I didn't sleep too well last night so I'm not sure."

After a few conversational niceties, Raspin got her talking about the old days. "You've been a widow for a long time," he said kindly.

"Yes," she said. "How long has it been? Charlie was fifteen or so when his father died."

"That's too bad. You both must have felt quite a loss, Charlie being so young."

"He was young, but he was a big boy. A tall boy. People always thought he was older than he was because he was so big, and he had quite a vocabulary. He talked like he was older, even back when he was a Cub Scout. Other kids didn't like that, I don't think. They didn't like the same things, the same games. He always had his own little hobbies. He stayed in his room a lot, building radios and so forth. He was always on his computer doing I don't know what. He said he was teaching himself coding, whatever that might be."

Raspin nudged the conversation along, encouraging Mrs. Crane to lose herself in the past.

"Where were you when your husband died?"

"Here. In the house. Maybe in bed. It was so long ago."

"How did you learn of his death?"

"Oh, I had to go out to the garage for something, we kept cases of soft drinks out there. My husband had a refrigerator in the garage for beer. And there he was. On the floor. Cold and stiff."

"How did Charlie take it?"

"Oh, he was at school. He stayed late for Computer Club. We didn't tell him until he came home. By then, his father was already at MacGiven's Funeral Home over on South Elm."

"What did the police say?"

"Oh, I don't remember. I was so upset. My neighbor came, and she helped me. I didn't know which way to turn, what to do. She helped me pick out his suit for the undertaker."

"Did the police say anything that you can recall?"

"I got the idea that it wasn't the first time they'd seen a man dead in his garage."

She looked frail and tired, and her thoughts seemed to have moved away from the past. Raspin thought he hadn't really learned much of anything new. He thanked her for the iced tea and stood to go.

"I wonder if I'm going to get any grandchildren before I die?" she said softly. "Charlie said he's going to bring home his bride for me to meet."

"A bride?" Raspin asked, suddenly alert.

"That's what my son said. I don't know if I believe him."

Interesting, Raspin thought. He pulled out his cell phone to call Joel as he walked back to where his car was parked.

Charlie pulled up a short while later after what he felt was his best practice session so far at the gun range. It cost twenty dollars an hour to shoot, plus a few dollars more for the recommended ear and eye protection and the paper targets. He felt ready. He felt strong.

"How are *you* feeling, Mother? All ready for lunch?"

"Tuna fish sandwiches sound good to me," she said.

They ate on the covered front porch and waved to neighbors passing by. Charlie liked for people to see him at home with his mother in between his trips down to the Keys. Everybody could see that she was being well taken care of. Everything was fine.

"Do you think I'll ever have grandchildren?" she asked.

Charlie looked at her curiously. "What made you think of that?"

"You told me you were going to bring home a bride. That I was going to meet her. That she was going to live here."

Her memory was sharper than he sometimes gave her credit for. Had he really said all that out loud? Sometimes, he got confused about what he said aloud and what he was just entertaining in his thoughts.

"Yes, Mother, you will be meeting her soon. I think I'll go down to get her and bring her back in the next day or two. Right after I take you to see Dr. Geiger for your cardiology appointment on Monday. We'll see how that goes, and then I'll be off."

Chapter 38
I Need to Tell You Something

Joel was in the kitchen when Carmella heard his cell phone receive a message. He used a 'whoosh' sound for his text signal. She glanced down at the phone on his bureau, thinking it might be from her brother about their day on the boat.

It was from a **Catherine**. She and **Kate** wanted to go back home tomorrow. Did Joel think it would be OK?

They were two women whose duplex in Marathon had been targeted by a dangerous suspect in a Key West murder, Joel explained. They had spent the weekend somewhere else and wanted to know if it was safe to go back to their place.

"Is it safe?"

"I don't know yet. I'm waiting for a call from upstate about the results of an investigation."

Carmella shrugged. "I hope everything works out."

Another text came. **Kate's grandfather wants a definitive answer.**

"Who is Kate's grandfather?" Carmella asked. "Some nerve, huh?"

"He's someone who is used to getting answers," Joel said.

"Oh, yeah? Some big shot?"

"You could say that. He's a former governor of Florida."

"Oh my gosh! Exciting!"

Joel shook his head. "Not exciting. The situation is not resolved yet, not at all. It would be best if he didn't insert himself into the investigation."

"Yeah," Carmella said. "Good luck with that."

She went out to sit by the pool with a glass of wine and her cell phone.

Joel telephoned up to Pasco. "Sorry I'm calling so late."

Dave Raspin reported that he had been out to see Mrs. Crane. Unfortunately, he had learned nothing definitive. She did indicate that her son was there in Pasco, although he was not actually at home during the time of Dave's house call. "I didn't get eyes on him. But she mentioned 'a bride'."

Joel texted Catherine back. **Charlie is confirmed in Dade City. Don't know for how long. Be careful. The suspects in the other matter are in custody, as I am sure Kate's grandfather knows. All the best—J.**

Joel joined Carmella outside. She was sitting on the concrete pool deck with her feet dangling in the warm water. He sat down beside her. The night air was a perfect temperature. For once, there was no neighborhood music or loud talk drifting into their little oasis.

"I need to tell you something," Joel began.

"Uh-oh," Carmella said. "That's how you begin when it's bad."

"Do I?" Joel said. "Thanks for letting me know. I'll try not to do it again. This isn't bad, but it's something I want you to know."

"OK."

"One of the women involved in the case I'm working on I knew before."

"Oh my gosh! You know the governor's granddaughter?"

"No, not her. The other one. Her neighbor next door."

"Oh, yeah?" Carmella said. "So...."

"I had an affair with her. A long time ago."

"How long?"

"Before you and I ever went out for the first time."

Carmella looked like she'd been hit with a brick. "How come you didn't tell me this until now?"

Joel shrugged.

He looks very uncomfortable, Carmella thought.

"I didn't think the case would ever get this complicated. I thought it would wrap up and be over."

"Who is she?"

"Her name is Catherine Cameron. She lived in Tampa for the past few years. She just moved down to the Keys."

"All this time you've kept in contact with her?"

Joel shook his head. "No contact at all. I saw her for the first time in twenty years on a police call to her house."

Carmela visibly relaxed. "Can I meet her?"

Joel shrugged. "Possibly when the case is over."

The only answer he could give, Carmela thought.

Joel stood up, water from the pool dripping down his legs. "I'm going to get ready for bed. Coming?"

"In a little while. I'm going to finish my wine. It's nice out here."

As soon as she heard the shower go on in the master bath, Carmella Googled 'Catherine Cameron.' It was a fairly common name, so there were a lot of hits. She tried 'Catherine Cameron+Tampa.' After a little bit of scrolling, she found a couple of mentions, including an article about Catherine's late husband, who had once run for political office up in Tampa. There was a black and white photo with the story. You can't tell much from an old newspaper picture, thought Carmella, but I can see that she's a good-looking blond girl.

Carmella decided to sleep on it. She wanted to figure out how she felt about it herself before she told anyone else.

Carmella called Emil in the morning as soon as Joel left for the Keys.

"It's 6:30 in the morning, Chica. What's up?"

"It's about Joel."

"What's my superstar brother done this time?" He yawned loudly, and his phone slipped to the floor. "Sorry. Now, what?"

"I found out that he's working on a case with an ex-girlfriend."

"He's got a cop for an ex-girlfriend? Really? How ex?"

"Not a cop. Just a girl. From a long time ago."

"So?"

Emil's casual response stopped Carmella. "What do you think I should do?"

"Nothing. Why, Carmella, what do *you* think you should do?"

"I don't know. I just thought you'd find it interesting."

"I might, if I knew more about it. Who's the woman?"

"Her name is Catherine Cameron. From Tampa."

"Never heard of her."

"He never mentioned anyone like that to you a long time ago, like twenty years?"

"Doesn't ring a bell. Not that I'd remember. Why is this a big deal?"

Carmella didn't respond.

"You still there?"

"Yes. I guess I thought you would want to know about it. That's all."

"Ah. So....is Joel's little side piece supposed to make what you and I've been up to okay? Like, Even-Steven?"

"No. Well, maybe in a way."

Chapter 39
Kill The Cop. Kill Someone.

Catherine and Kate left Joel's cottage and were back at the duplex before ten in the morning. With Rocky settled back inside safely, the two women left for their jobs.

Kate had a home security installation scheduled up on Conch Key.

"I don't know how long this is going to take me. The guy sounds super-picky and super-indecisive. The worst kind."

***

Charlie's trip back down to the Keys from Dade City was no fun at all. The traffic, even on the roads he used in the middle of the state, was heavy. He wasn't exactly sure how to carry out his plan. Sometimes he thought he would feel happy again and totally free from all his misery if he just knew that Catherine was dead. She would never be with another man. The cop wouldn't be able to have her.

He also thought about trying to find out first if she would just go voluntarily with him back up to Dade City. It had been a long time, weeks and weeks, since they'd even spoken. She could have had a change of heart. She might be thinking about all the good times they'd had together in Tampa.

He wondered if she had figured out who'd taken her clothes and the other things from her apartment. Maybe she hadn't even noticed. Maybe she had spent the whole time he had been away in Dade City naked in bed with the cop.

Charlie pulled over to the side of the road. He cried for almost ten minutes, loudly, with the windows rolled up.

Kill the cop. Kill Catherine. Kill himself.

Kill the cop. Make Catherine watch. Kill Catherine.

Have sex with Catherine. Make the cop watch. Kill Catherine.

Screw it. The original plan was the best plan. Take Catherine to Dade City. Put her downstairs. Dress her in the wedding gown. Have one wedding night after another after another until she was pregnant.

His mother could teach her how to cook his food the way he liked it.

They would raise their kids the way he had been raised.

Chapter 40

Carmella and Joel and Charlie and Catherine

Carmella looked at her reflection in the bathroom mirror. Her eyes were puffy, like she'd been crying, only she hadn't been. Emil said it was probably the alcohol. He ought to know.

She went out to the kitchen. Joel must have cleaned it up before he'd left for work. She poured herself a vodka and orange juice. Breakfast of champions. My husband is having an affair, she said aloud to herself.

"You don't know that," replied Emil when she called him again. "And you aren't doing yourself any favors, hitting the sauce."

"Can you come over?"

"I can't. I have to work today."

Carmella hung up and sobbed. I' a forty-something failure in real estate sales whose husband is screwing around. She made herself another drink, this time a vodka on the rocks. She went out to the pool with her cell phone and searched for more information about Catherine Cameron. Nothing came up that wasn't related to Catherine's late husband.

"What would *I* do if I was a widow?" Carmella asked aloud. As a law enforcement officer's wife, it wasn't the first time she'd considered the question. 'If I had a dollar for every time I panicked when the telephone rang when Joel was out on patrol duty, I'd be rich,' Carmella used to say to the other police wives. Today, the thought of Joel being killed on the job just made her feel numb. Maybe it was the vodka, she thought, taking another sip.

Joel was clear with himself that he hadn't been honest with Carmella. Catherine wasn't just a job to him. She wasn't just a woman he'd dated in the distant past. They'd resumed their past romance, only now it was considered an "affair" because he was married, and he didn't know what to do about it. He wanted Catherine, and he didn't want to hurt either Carmella or Catherine. Unfortunately, by this point, it was pretty much guaranteed that one or both or all three of them would be hurt. He could spare his wife if he and Catherine didn't see each other again after Catherine's stalker case was wrapped up. But he couldn't spare himself no matter what he did.

He arrived home before five o'clock. Carmella was asleep on a chaise lounge by the pool. Her mouth was open, and she was snoring. Joel picked up the glass by the table near her and sniffed it. Should he let her sleep it off, or try to rouse her?

"Carmella," he said, shaking her gently. "Carmella, wake up."

"What are you doing here?" she asked groggily.

"I decided to come home. I took off a little early."

He looked her over Puffy eyes. Disheveled. This was not Carmella's style. "What's the matter? Did something happen?"

"Why do you care? You've been so busy down there in the Keys with your girlfriend." She looked at him defiantly.

Joel didn't say anything. He knew not to get into a discussion with an intoxicated person. He went inside to fix dinner for them. He'd grill some hamburgers and make a salad.

Later, about nine o'clock, Carmella was sufficiently sober to talk. "I'm sorry I was such a mess when you came home. How was your day? How is the girl?"

"She's safe for now, but it's not over. It won't be over until the guy is apprehended."

"Will it be over then?" she asked.

Joel looked her square in the eye. "I don't know. I hope so."

***

Charlie finally arrived back down in the Keys and got to his motel just as the sky was turning dark. It was inky blue with some mean clouds piling up. Probably rain soon. Maybe thunder. That would be good in some ways.

He unlocked the door to his room. It appeared neat and undisturbed. The house cleaner had been there with fresh towels at least once. He walked over to the office.

"I'm going to be checking out. I just wanted to let you know, and to settle up my account." It was going to be a big bill, but he had planned for that. He would pay the balance with a wad of cash he'd brought down. A fake name. No paper trail.

Things were in motion, and they couldn't be stopped. The train was starting to roll down the incline, and the brakes were off. Good, he thought. I'm ready.

***

Carmella's phone chimed while she was in the shower. Joel glanced at it. A text from Emil.

Hi, Babe. Sorry I couldn't talk earlier. Hope you're feeling better. We'll get together again soon. Can't wait to get my hands on you. XOXOXO

"You got a text from my brother," Joel said when Carmella came out of the bathroom.

Joel rarely looked at Carmella's phone, and Carmella seldom left her phone out. Periodically, she deleted any messages from Emil. By now, it was close to a twenty-year habit. Maybe more.

"Oh, yeah?" she said, as casually as she could. "What did he say?"

Joel handed her the phone. Carmella looked at the message and shrugged. "That's just Emil being Emil."

"Was something bothering you? Anything I can help you with?" The expression in his light blue eyes was open and calm, but shrewd. That cop mind of his never quit.

"It was nothing. The pool pump was messed up I fixed it by turning it off and then back on again. It wasn't sucking." She shouldn't have said that. It was a true statement... but a while ago. And if Joel asked Emil about it, she wasn't sure Emil would remember or understand what to say.

What would she do if Joel left her? She was pretty sure he would. He would start wondering how long it had been going on, when did it start, and she had no doubt he would figure it out. Their marriage would be over. She didn't know if Emil would come through for her if that happened.

Joel was her husband, and she was not going to just hand him over to this Catherine.

First thing tomorrow, I'm going to get back to the gym, get my hair done, and maybe get some new clothes. Order some sexy underwear from the catalog. Tire him out in bed so that there's nothing left to take down to the Keys.

She put on a sheer red negligee and walked out to where Joel was sitting in his office space. "Are you coming to bed?"

He barely looked up. "In a little while."

He waited until she seemed like she was asleep, and texted Emil.

We need to talk. Are you at home?

After a while, Emil texted back.

Can it wait? I have someone here.

Joel didn't bother to respond. He got into his personal vehicle and headed over to Emil's apartment. He left his service weapon secured at home. We need to talk, little brother, but I don't want to take any chances. No way I'm going to prison over your very sorry ass.

He felt as if, out of the ether, some pieces had slipped into place in his mind.

When he had come home from Iraq long ago, he'd had a feeling about Carmella and Emil, but he just didn't want to know. He was looking forward to a calm, happy, stable family life after the dust and the brutality and the loneliness. He hadn't been motivated to know. He'd been away for a long time, at least a long time for someone with Carmella's disposition. Carmella needed a lot of emotional support, especially when she had been younger. They weren't married back then, or even technically engaged. He'd bought her a diamond ring when he'd been on leave in Bahrain and gave it to her when he got home. She'd loved it.

Emil was weak, too. He needed women to prop up his self-esteem, and he always had, beginning with their mother.

All the pieces that Joel had never chosen to carefully examine or to put together had fallen in to place in his mind. But I have to know for sure, Joel thought. He didn't permit himself to think deeply about the other part, the part about why he was allowing himself to look closely at his marriage now, the part about Catherine and him.

Chapter 41

When Was the Last Time?

Sometime before nine, Catherine heard a car pull up to the duplex, reverse, and back into her driveway.

Kate must be home, she thought. I guess she decided not to work any later than this.

There was a knock on the door. Her side. Not Kate's. Catherine cautiously opened it. No one was there. A dark sedan had backed up almost to the front stoop. The large trunk was wide open and empty.

The screen door on the ocean side scraped slightly, and she turned to see a loomingly tall man striding across the room directly to her. He had on a black and white ski mask, like a death's head. She pivoted to run out the front door but was blocked by the car. Terror set her heart pounding. She grabbed the broom by the door and swung it hard. The space was too small to achieve much force. She landed a glancing blow on the man's leg. He grunted as he grabbed her arms, turned her, and pulled them tightly behind her. She shrieked, but it came out sounding to her like a mouse's squeaking as the cat's paw comes down on its little neck.

Her hands were roughly zip-tied behind her, and she was shoved forward, out the door, and into the trunk of the car. She felt wetness and inhaled the chloroform before she could stop herself. She heard the trunk lid slam closed as she blacked out.

When Kate arrived home two hours later, she noticed that Catherine's front door was ajar, but she didn't think anything of it at the time. She got right to work on her laptop, monitoring some new setups she had running up the Keys. It was only when she heard a cat crying and saw Rocky outside at her screened door that she got up to check on her neighbor.

After some time, Catherine regained consciousness in the dark trunk of a moving vehicle. Her head hurt. Her shoulders hurt. She thought about who had taken her captive. It had to be Charlie. He was the right height and build, although perhaps leaner than she recalled.

She shifted around, trying to get her arms worked into a more comfortable position behind her back. She pulled her knees up in a fetal position so she could maybe manage to work her feet back through the flex-cuffs that held her wrists. That way, at least her hands would be in front of her. She willed herself think of it as trying to master a new yoga *asana*, not as trying to escape from the clutches of a psychopath. Inhale. Exhale. Crunch. Knees up even higher. Inhale. Exhale. Work the feet through.

I hope Rocky's OK, she thought. I hope Kate gets home soon and figures out what happened to me and calls the cops. I hope Joel can give them some information that will help them find me.

How should I act with Charlie so I can stay alive? She was pretty sure she knew what he wanted.

She felt the car pick up speed. Could they already be off the Keys and on the Florida Turnpike? Catherine wondered at his choice of travel route. The toll-by-plate feature of the turnpike, or the transponder he might have purchased, could potentially enable law enforcement to learn what route he had taken and even his approximate location. As if her thoughts had been read, the car slowed to exit, and then continued at a variable rate of speed with occasional stops. Traffic lights, she guessed.

Catherine lay in the dark trunk breathing the stale air, hoping not too much carbon monoxide was seeping in, as she continued to try to work her way out of the plastic cuffs. They seemed to have a locking mechanism, like regular zip ties. Maybe they were. That "lock," probably, was their weakest point. She couldn't make out anything in the near darkness. A bit of a red glow seemed to light the space intermittently, apparently when the brakes were being applied. She felt around the trunk as best as she could for something sharp.

***

Joel arrived at the apartment building in West Miami where his brother had been renting a place since his most recent divorce and pressed the buzzer. He didn't wait for the elevator in the fake marble lobby. He took the stairs to Emil's floor, composed himself, and knocked lightly.

"Go away!" a girl giggled. "We don't want any!"

Joel rapped on the door more authoritatively. He heard the security chain slip off, and Emil opened the door.

"Big brother! A surprise! Come in."

Emil gestured to the barely clad young woman with his head, and she scooted off to the bedroom.

"Can I get you something to drink?"

Joel shook his head and stood facing his brother.

"Sit down. Take a load off." Emil's wary look was in sharp contrast to his jovial words and gestures. Joel waited.

"Honey, something's come up," he called back. "How about if we get together another time soon?"

The woman, a small blond perhaps in her late twenties, took the hint and walked quickly out of the apartment carrying her espadrille platform sandals. Joel thought she looked a little like Dawn, Emil's most recent ex-wife, but younger. It was mainly her tawny blond shag, and her grin, Joel thought. Dawn had a nice smile, too.

"So," Emil said. He had made a guess as to the purpose of Joel's visit. Carmella had gotten drunk and spilled the beans. How much did Joel know? What could he still lie about to maybe try to salvage something?

"I want to hear your side of it," Joel began.

Clever opening gambit, thought Emil. I have no idea what Carmella did or did not say to him. She'd been kind of emotionally unstable lately, so there was no telling. His phone vibrated in his pocket. A text. He wished he could look at it.

Maybe she was sending him some background information, something for him to use to his benefit here. As it was, he felt like he was trying to land a plane in the fog with no navigation Intel.

"May I assume we are talking about Carmella here?"

Joel nodded.

"We've been friends for a long time, since high school. We talk pretty often, on and off. You know all that."

Joel nodded again.

What else did he know? Emil decided to continue in the pseudo-frankness mode and try to figure out what to say next as the conversation progressed.

"I've been friends with Carmella forever. We talk on the phone sometimes, like I said, and we text. Once in a while, I come over if she calls and needs help with something. When you're away. It's been like that ever since you were over in Iraq. Twenty, twenty-five years?"

"Did you fuck her?"

Emil shook his head. "We're just friends."

Joel stood up abruptly. Emil braced himself for a punch, but Joel turned on his heel and left the apartment.

I should call Carmella, Emil thought. Tell her to delete any texts she might have saved. He made the call, but it went to voice mail, so he didn't say anything. Fuck. He's going to tell her that I talked.

When Joel got home, the house was straightened up and Carmella had changed into a t-shirt and jeans. Girded for battle, Joel thought.

"When was the last time?" Joel asked her.

Carmella stood very still. He could tell that she was trying to decide what Emil had said.

"I'm not sure what you're talking about."

"What you mean is you're not sure what I know. If he hasn't already told you, I was just over at Emil's."

Carmella shrugged. Her signature move, Joel thought. "We're friends. You know that."

"When was the last time?" Joel repeated.

Carmella said nothing. Joel went into the bedroom to pack some clean clothes. He was driving back to the Keys tonight, regardless.

"It was never anything," Carmella said, following him.

"If I knew all the details, every single last one...do you think I would agree that your relationship with my brother was 'never anything'?" he asked. "Just out of curiosity, when *was* the last time?"

Carmella was silent.

"Huh." Joel said. "That recently."

"I know why you're walking out instead of trying to fix things between us," Carmella said, following him out to the driveway.

"Here's your perfect excuse to go with that Catherine. You don't want to fix things."

"We'll see - to use one of your favorite expressions." Joel gave her a light peck on the cheek. "Take care of yourself. I'll be in touch."

As Joel started the commute down to his rented cottage, he kept suppressing the urge to call Catherine and tell her that he needed to see her. When he hit a Key Largo traffic signal, he had his cell phone in his hand, but he knew the best thing to do, the right thing to do, was to take some time by himself sorting out his feelings. He wasn't due back on the job until seven in the morning, so he could have the night alone with his thoughts. The isolation would give him hours to reflect on what Carmela had thrown at him. *Was* he looking at her infidelity as an easy excuse to justify his own? To ensure he would be less tempted to call Catherine, he turned off his phone and put it away.

He was awakened before the night sky was showing gray in the east by loud pounding on his door and a woman shouting, "Joel! Sheriff Joel! Wake up!"

Kate was on the front stoop of the cottage in shorts and a tee-shirt, jumping up and down.

"Catherine's gone! I think Charlie came and took her!"

"Did you call it in?" Joel asked, grabbing his phone. "To the county sheriff?"

"For sure! They came and took the information, but it seemed like it was, like, 'whatever,' to them. Can you do anything?"

"Can you give me your best estimate as far as the time parameters?"

"I worked until midnight, maybe. Then, quite a while after I got home, I heard her cat crying outside, so I got him, brought him over, and her door was open and stuff was messed up in her apartment, like there was a fight. So, I called the cops, and they came over and made a report. Didn't you hear about it?"

Joel shook his head. "I wasn't on duty, and I had my phone off."

Raspin, up in Pasco County, was already awake for the day and took Joel's call. "I'll get somebody over there and try to get a warrant to search the premises. That's a big, old house. One of not too many in Florida that probably has a basement of some kind. There's a garage, and I think a shed out back. I'm quite sure that the only residents since the father died are Mr. Crane and his mother. She's eighty if she's a day."

Joel was silent, the weight of the situation leaving him temporarily without words. Finally, he said, "The guy's unhinged. I'm going to request personal time and drive up."

Chapter 42
Is That a Crime?

Charlie made the drive back home to Dade City with only one stop for fuel and refreshments. He chose a gas station on an isolated stretch of Highway 27 and paid with cash. He thought about offering Catherine some water but decided not to take any risks. He wanted to get her to the house before the sun rose if he could. She wouldn't die of thirst before then.

The sky was turning gray with the impending dawn as he pulled on to his street. Who among his nosy neighbors would be up and about, walking their little mutts? Mrs. Speer would for sure have the white poodle mix out early. He slowly drove around the block to Cedar Grove Street and parked at the curb in front of the house directly behind his. Mrs. Cargill never had a light on or the shades up until 8:30 at the earliest.

Getting Catherine into his house was a problem he solved by loading her from the trunk directly into a large wheelbarrow from his backyard shed and pushing her though the narrow gate his yard shared with the Cargill property. She was out cold, thanks to a jab with his needle.

It was quite a trick to balance and push the wheelbarrow across the damp grass. It needed mowing again. Always something. He unlocked and opened the outside basement bulkhead doors and pulled Catherine down the five steps to the inside as carefully as he could. She'd gotten pretty dirty on the trip, and maybe a little bruised, but no permanent damage.

Once inside, he tied her to the bed. She needed a bath, definitely, and some clean clothes. Maybe some food, and of course, the toilet. He had everything pretty much prepared. As usual, his plans were turning out perfectly.

Charlie secured the bulkhead opening and made his way back across the back yard to move his car around the block to the front of the house.

He parked and waved to Mr. Smith, who had just come out to pick up his newspaper. Inside, the house was quiet. He started the coffee pot and washed up and shaved in the downstairs guest bathroom. Any unexpected visitors would see him as an early riser, in control, and calmly reading the paper and having a cup of coffee on his front porch.

He didn't have long to wait. Charlie had barely finished reading the first section of the paper when a white county sheriff's vehicle pulled up. Charlie stood up, feeling confident.

"Sheriff Raspin. You're up early. What can I do for you?"

Raspin looked around. The house was quiet, and the porch was coated with the morning dew. Birds flitted around a bird feeder hanging from a hook at the far end. Charlie looked like he'd just had a shower. His hair was still damp.

"I came by to see how your mother is doing. Last time I checked in, she seemed like she was a little unclear about your whereabouts."

"Is that a crime? Being old and confused?"

"Of course not. Checking on the welfare of our elderly citizens is a part of our public service that we like to do when we can. Especially since you seem to have been gone quite a bit lately."

Charlie shrugged. "I'm here. All's well."

Raspin turned to leave. As he stepped down to the front walkway, Mrs. Crane called down loudly from upstairs, "Charlie, are you home? Can you bring me some coffee? Is your bride here?"

Charlie looked at Raspin and shrugged nonchalantly. "It's hell getting old, isn't it?"

Raspin nodded and left.

Chapter 43
You Made Me Do This

Catherine's head ached, and she felt nauseous from whatever had been in the syringe Charlie had poked her with. Her mouth was fuzzy, and her legs felt rubbery. She was as weak as she'd ever been, worse than the flu or any other illness she'd ever had.

The bulkhead door opened, and Charlie came down. He was clean-shaven and dressed in shorts and a polo shirt. He could be going to play tennis or out for a morning of errands.

He looked her over. "Are you still sick?"

Catherine decided to try a show of strength. "What do you think?" she said coldly. "You drugged me, you threw me in a car trunk, and dragged me down here. I need to pee, shower, and eat something."

Charlie smiled. "That's my feisty girl. No wonder I love you so much."

He pointed to the toilet and shower. "Have at it. Want me to wash your back?"

She stared at him, waiting for him to leave. Finally, he stood up.

"We have a busy, busy schedule today. Make yourself clean and pretty."

"What are you going to do?"

"You'll find out. Don't make any noise, or I'll have to gag you and tie you to the bed. Here's some clothes."

He tossed her a set of her laciest lingerie and a clean pair of shorts and a tee shirt from a drawer.

"Those are my clothes."

"Yes, I brought them here a couple of weeks ago from the apartment you used to live in."

Catherine noted his use of the past tense. He'd been in the duplex before he'd kidnapped her. He'd planned this for a long time.

"Where's my cat?"

"He's fine. Probably. I left the door open. Your neighbor will take care of him. I didn't leave her a note or anything, but a smart girl like her will figure out that you've gone. We wouldn't want anything to happen to a nice cat like Rocky, would we?"

Catherine looked around the room. The heavy bulkhead door seemed to be the only way out. The small, high window might allow a little child or a cat egress, but not her. She wished she felt stronger.

"Why did you bring me here?" She intuitively avoided the word 'kidnap.'

"You'll find out. Don't make any noise, or I'll have to gag you and handcuff you to the bed," he repeated sternly, "until you get some sense into that pretty head."

The bondage seemed to be a recurring theme, his fantasy or his delusion, Catherine noted.

Charlie looked around the room, appraising the decor.

"I really don't want to have our wedding night down here, do you? There's such a nice room that I made for us upstairs. Can you try to relax? No noise. No fighting. Ever since I met you, I've been trying to get you to like me. Can you just settle down and try to understand that?"

Footsteps on a squeaky wood floor overhead caught Catherine's attention. She looked at Charlie.

"My mother. She lives with us. I've told her quite a bit about you. She knows you're my chosen bride."

Charlie looked at the clothing Catherine was wearing. "Now that I think of it, you'd better change into something more modest for her. She doesn't like to see women in shorts. She thinks women look cheap in them." He selected one of the sundresses he'd brought from her place in the Keys and held it up.

Catherine sat on the bed, refusing to move.

"Are you trying to tempt me?" Charlie asked playfully. "Is that what this is? Do you want me to take off your clothes for you? Strip you naked even before our wedding? I've been wanting to do that for a long time, but I've been respectful.

Remember in Tampa? We were kissing in your bedroom. I wanted you so much that night." His voice grew angry. "But you said 'no' and I stopped. I've waited very patiently, very respectfully while you played hard to get. The time for that is over. Unless you prefer it that way? Do you want me to rip your clothes off?"

He was staring at her breasts under her tee shirt. Catherine's eyes dropped to the bulge in his pants, and she turned her head away. "I'll dress myself when you leave the room."

Charlie mock bowed. "I'll leave you to it, then. My mother is expecting you."

Upstairs, Charlie brought his mother a cup of tea and helped her get settled in her lounge chair.

"Catherine seems just about ready to meet you," he said.

"Is that girl here of her own free will?" Mrs. Crane asked peevishly. "The sheriff will cause us some more trouble if she isn't. He said he'd be back."

"Raspin is a moron," replied Charlie. "He couldn't even figure out a kindergarten puzzle with his very small endowment of brains. You know that, don't you?"

"I don't think he was the sheriff back then, was he? That was a long time ago." She took a sip of her tea. "Do you want him to arrest you? To finally put a stop to everything? That's not what I want. I'd be all alone here. I don't think I could manage. Don't tempt fate, Son."

"Mother," Charlie explained patiently, "I have the whole thing planned. Don't you want a grand baby before you go? You used to say you how much you wished you had grandchildren. Well, now that Catherine's here, you'll finally have one. More than one, maybe. I want to be a father. Or, maybe I just really, really want to make a baby with her. I'll keep trying until it happens."

Mrs. Crane shook her head. "I don't know about this. I don't think you realize what could happen if that woman is here against her will." She sighed. "But I do want grandchildren. It makes it easier to accept that your own time is about up, I think."

"I always keep my promises to you, you know that. I've taken the very best of care of you." He paused, looking into her eyes. "Even though you really let me down sometimes when I was young."

She sighed again. "What could I do? You were too small to remember, but whenever I tried to stop him, it just made him angrier. It was worse for both of us."

"You never really tried to stop it. Not that I saw."

"I did try. I tried my best."

"You could have divorced him. Why did you stay?"

"He said he'd kill both me and you both if I tried to leave, and I had no reason to doubt him. Divorce wasn't easy back then like it is now. Was it really so bad for you? I don't remember it that way. Can't you please just try to put everything in the past so we can go on with our lives?"

"Sometimes I'm afraid that it ruined me, Mother. Do you think I'm a good boy, a good son?" He sat down beside her. "Can you just tell me that, Mother? Please?"

Mrs. Crane stared past him, to the dining room table that Charlie had set for the wedding reception. "That cake looks good. I think I'd like a piece, with another cup of tea."

Charlie stood up. "You'll need to wait for just a bit. The cake is for the reception. It's time to get started. I'll go get Catherine. I'll do you both the courtesy of a brief premarital introduction."

Charlie forced Catherine, gagged, hands tied behind her back, up the bulkhead steps and in through the kitchen side door.

"Here she is, Mother." He took her gag off. "Meet Miss Catherine Cameron, my fiancée. See, I told you she was real."

Mrs. Crane stared at the disheveled blond woman.

"She isn't a young as I'd hoped she'd be. Can she still give me a grand baby?"

"She can, I think. But, to your point, we'll have to get started right away." Charlie steadied Catherine, who was still a little woozy. "Isn't she beautiful?"

"She looks angry. Why is she tied up? Is that the only way you could get her to come?"

"She's always liked to play a little hard to get with me, is all. She'll settle down and stop playing games after the wedding. Once I've made her mine."

Chapter 44

Charlie's Fantasy Life

Charlie returned Catherine to the basement through the bulkhead door and untied her.

"You'll be happy to know I bought a few more things for our wedding reception. Champagne and flowers. I ran down to the supermarket this morning. Our wedding cake, which I also picked up, isn't anything fancy or personalized, but our guest list is so small it shouldn't matter. I chose a chocolate cake with white icing and pink flowers. My mother loves chocolate. I bet you do, too. Who doesn't?"

He pulled the wedding gown he'd bought at the Key Largo resale shop from the closet. "I hope this is to your liking."

Catherine stared at the dress.

"Beautiful, isn't it? Here's the veil, and possibly Mother can weave a crown of daisies for you, if you'd like. I think it will be okay for a casual wedding."

Charlie looked carefully at Catherine. "You need to do your part. You need to wash your hair, fix it nice, and put on some makeup. All your stuff is in the bathroom."

Catherine folded her arms and said, "None of this is going to happen the way you think it is. You're plowing ahead with your delusional plans, but there's a fundamental problem you keep overlooking. I don't want to marry you. I never implied otherwise. I moved four hundred miles to get away from you. You stalked me all the way down to the Keys. How did you even know I was there?"

"Your friend at your job in Tampa told me, Tanya is her name, I think?"

"You drugged me. You kidnapped me," Catherine went on. "If you wanted a relationship with me, why not try to go about it in a normal way?"

"Oh, I did. I really, really tried. And you know I did I was nice. I invited you on dates. I helped fix your house. I brought you food. I was friendly to your cat. I never once forced myself on you. And what did you do in return? You called the cops and then moved away. So, I did what any normal man would do. I followed the girl of my dreams to get her back."

Catherine sighed. "Charlie, I am so sorry if you think I was leading you on at any point. My husband had died. You offered to help me. You were nice to me. I enjoyed your company, at least until you started getting obsessive. But I just wasn't ready for a relationship, like I told you. Repeatedly. Why can't you accept that?"

He smiled grimly. "Because I know you let the cop have you. He spent the night. You seemed to be very ready for a relationship with him. You let him do whatever he wanted. I saw it. It broke my heart. But now it's my turn. You're going to be mine, from this day forward. Till death do us part."

Catherine rolled her eyes and looked past Charlie. She made a dash for the steps leading out through the bulkhead to the back yard. Charlie reached up and grabbed her ankle as she reached the top step. She kicked him hard in the face with her other foot, bloodying his nose, but he overpowered her and pulled her back down into the basement room.

"If you do that again...." There was cold menace in his voice. His eyes were a frozen blue. He had slipped into another persona, this one a looming, vengeful brute. He drew his hand back and slapped her face. His eyes gleamed with a hard, angry purpose. His face and his voice had changed into something unrecognizable.

"Charlie! Charlie Crane! Stop it! Charlie, stop!" she screamed. "I don't want any of this. Stop it, Charlie!"

"You're making me do it. You forced me to. It's your fault. Now it's going to be Charlie's turn to get what *he* wants." He pulled himself off her, panting.

"I need for you to get up and accompany me all the way to the top floor of our house to our bridal suite," he said in a calmer voice. "There's good light up there, which we will need for our home movies."

He gagged her again and tied her arms and dragged her off the basement bed and pushed her roughly up the steps out of the bulkhead, and then up the back stairway of the house all the way to the third floor.

The bedroom suite was bright and spacious with vintage details. The bed was a mahogany four-poster piled with white bedding. The wide-plank wood floor was bare. Tall mirrors reflected the window light.

Catherine noticed the black leather mattress restraints just as Charlie pushed her down on to the bed. He quickly secured her wrists and ankles to the bed posts and cut off what remained of her clothing. He stood staring at her body.

Catherine turned her eyes away from his pants. "Oh, for god's sake," she swore under her breath.

Charlie laid the wedding dress and veil out at the bottom of the bed.

He retrieved three professional-looking video cameras on tripods from the corner and attached them to a laptop. He positioned the cameras and tested the sound, the video feeds, and the lighting.

"You are about to become a star among a certain population segment," he announced.

"I have everything perfectly set up for the main event," he went on in a matter-of-fact tone. "I've completely researched and tested how to live stream pay-per-view and automatically process payments and consumer access. I have advertised the approximate start time, and the reservations and payments have been pouring in. Seems like a lot of the world on the dark web wants to see *The Reluctant Bride.* You're going to become the main attraction of the show pretty soon," he smirked, holding up a large vibrator and a black leather Lone

Ranger mask he'd pulled out of a drawer, "and you're going to make us some serious money tonight."

"So, this is how it's going to happen," he continued conversationally, as he walked around adjusting the lighting. "Later, after we have the champagne and cake downstairs, I'm going to video you and me up here on our wedding night. Mostly you. I'll be wearing this black leather mask you see here, both for the effect on the viewers and for my own anonymity. You'll start off wearing your wedding gown. I'm going to secure you to the bed again, pretty much like you are now. You'll seem a little tipsy from our celebratory wedding reception champagne," he continued, pointing to a wine cooler on the dresser. "Next, I'll slowly cut your white dress off for the camera, revealing that hot body of yours bit by bit to the worldwide network of bondage enthusiasts. I really hope thousands will be watching...and paying. The money mainly seems to be coming in from the middle east and Japan so far, but you can never tell for sure, which is the point. For all I know, it could be the guy down the street."

"Anyway, then, I'm going to attach these tight nipple clamps to your rosy little buds and tug on them until you start squirming," he said, holding up a pair of menacing-looking alligator clamps connected to each other by a decorative silver chain. "The main action will begin when I start working on you with this big boy vibrator," he said, holding it up. "I'll need you to scream for the camera. You probably won't be able to help yourself, but I won't stop with the vibrator until you give our viewership their money's worth. Then, I'm going to plow myself into you until I'm done. The program will finish with you being close to passed out from the extreme pleasure I've given you, and with a tight shot of my baby-making stuff dripping out of you."

"So, that's the condensed version of the script," he grinned. "Sounds like a dream wedding night to me. Plus, I'm going to make more money than I ever have in my life. Turns out, connoisseurs will pay serious cash on the dark market for this live stream, but it has to include certain elements, like extreme close ups of your face when you are coming repeatedly and involuntarily from the vibrator, and close-ups of all your body parts."

"They will be paying extra to watch me carefully bind and truss up your D-cup breasts with this silk cord." He held up a long coil of thin red rope. "I'm going to live-pierce your nipples with a sterilized needle while you are hand-cuffed to the bed and your breasts are jutting out from their red silk bindings and insert these little gold rings in each of them. We'll use ice cubes from the champagne bucket to numb them and get them really stiff for the piercing. There's a second set of rings for, um, down below. They are paying *way* extra for the close-in shot of that piercing, let me tell you. You'll always be wearing gold rings from now on, including, of course, your wedding ring. You'll never be allowed to forget whose property your body is, and I'll tug on them whenever you need a reminder, till death do us part."

"You'll have had to sign this release form," he went on, "outlining your full voluntary consent to participate in the video event, attesting that you are of legal age, and that you are participating in activities of a certain nature specified below of your own free will. Actually, I've already practiced your signature and signed your name. Pretty good job, huh?" He held up the form for her to see.

"Finally, when our wedding night's over, I'll send a free copy of the video of the entire pay-per-view event to your cop, as well as a copy of your signed consent form, so he'll know the entire world saw who won."

Charlie smiled down at Catherine. "I bet you never thought you'd be an international star among a certain clientele back when you signed the attendance sheet at that bromeliad society meeting. But I saw your potential right away and have been figuring out how to do what I always wanted to do to you, ever since."

"Well," he continued as he undid her bindings, "I guess it's about time for the wedding. What do you think, so far?" he asked, watching intently for her reaction.

Catherine sat up, yawned, and massaged her wrists. "I think you have the very active fantasy life of a forty-something year old guy who still lives with his mother."

Chapter 45
She's All Mine, Now

"Charlie," his mother called up the stairway. "Charles Crane! Can you hear me? When are we going to start this wedding? I am expecting my guest any minute now. You both need to get down here!"

"We're on our way," Charlie called back, his hands tightly gripping Catherine's arms as he guided her down the stairs ahead of him.

Catherine was now dressed in the thrift-shop wedding gown and veil. That's what she'd called it. She seemed almost amused, which bewildered him. He'd expected terror, the kind he remembered when he was a small child watching and listening to his father control his mother. His mother's fright had secretly, shamefully, thrilled him, and he'd envied the power his father had.

He'd felt humiliated by his own weakness when it had been his turn for one of the beatings. He didn't understand why Catherine seemed so casual after he'd briefed her on what was in store for her later. Maybe it was exactly what she wanted.

Pasco County Deputy Sheriff David Raspin parked in front of the Crane residence as Mrs. Crane's invited guest. He was dressed neatly in plain clothes but carried his holstered *SIG Sauer P320* in sight under his jacket.

Charlie glanced out at Raspin coming up the walk to the front door and went over to the sideboard where the cake and champagne were waiting. He took his new Taurus handgun out of the left top drawer from under the linen napkins that had belonged to his grandmother. He chambered a round and thrust the weapon into his waistband at his back.

"That's really stupid," observed Catherine. "No one carries a handgun that way in real life, unless they want to shoot their own ass off."

"Oh, so, screwing the cop made you an expert on guns," Charlie said.

"No," Catherine smirked, "but screwing the cop made me an expert on screwing."

Raspin tapped on the door and let himself in. "I hope I'm not too late."

Charlie snorted and handed him a champagne flute. "Sorry. Wedding ceremony, such as it was, is over. Now, it's time for the fun."

"Oh," said Raspin. "Where's the officiant? I must surely know him, if he's from around here. I'd like to say 'hi'."

Charlie smiled condescendingly. "We recited our vows privately. I wrote them. My mother's the witness. Catherine seemed to stumble a little on the 'obey' part. I had to give her a prompt."

"None of that happened," Catherine retorted.

Raspin saw an annoyed-looking woman dressed in a wedding gown that clearly was not a custom fit. One of her cheeks was swollen, but her eyes were alert. She had bruises on her wrists and arms. She seemed to be having difficulty keeping her balance.

"Don't mind her," Charlie said smoothly. "She's had too much champagne already."

"It's these crappy shoes," she snapped back, kicking them off. "You have terrible taste. Plus, who buys shoes from a thrift shop?"

Raspin scanned the room and glanced into the kitchen and living room.

"Yes," Charlie noticed. "It was a small wedding." He pulled Catherine to him. "We were just talking about how the really fun part is still ahead of us tonight."

Raspin saw the anger flare in Catherine's eyes. "Are you here of your own free choice?" he asked.

She shook her head. "In a word, 'no.' Charlie here is a delusional psychopath. I'm hoping your presence is a sign that I might get out of here alive."

"If you believe in free will, everything is a choice," Charlie said to Raspin. He squeezed Catherine's arm possessively. "She's all mine, now. The waiting was the hardest part. Tom Petty," he said with a wink.

"Do you have a properly executed marriage license?" Raspin asked.

"Sure," Charlie replied. He reached behind his back and pulled the Taurus 9mm out of his waist band. "This good?"

Joel wheeled in behind Raspin's sheriff's vehicle in time to hear the gunshot. He called 911 to report the address and the circumstances, and quickly made his way to a side door of the Victorian. He found Raspin sitting on the floor of the dining room, propped up against the wainscoting, bleeding from what appeared to be a shoulder wound. An old lady dressed in lavender and lace was standing nearby holding a piece of cake on a china plate.

"I just want grandchildren," she said timidly. "Did I do something wrong? Is that nice sheriff going to be okay? Would you like a piece of wedding cake?"

Chapter 46
I Told You They'd Come Someday

Joel slipped past Mrs. Crane, who continued to stare at him in confusion.

"Who are you, again?" she asked.

"I'm with the caterer," he said kindly. "Please take a seat at the table."

Charlie was grasping Catherine's right arm tightly with his left hand and was holding the Taurus with his right. He pushed her up the stairs. So intent was he in forcing his struggling bride up to his bridal suite that he paid no attention to what his mother was saying.

Catherine stumbled on the second-floor landing and caught a glimpse under her arm of Joel through the balusters a flight below with his back pressed against the staircase wall, his weapon drawn. Relief flooded her face, but she kept her focus on Charlie. She sat down on a stair and folded her arms.

"I'm not taking one more step up to your amateur-hour torture chamber. You'll have to carry me. A bride should be carried."

Charlie missed seeing her smirk, but it was for Joel.

"If you insist, Mrs. Crane." He tucked his weapon in his waistband.

Catherine rolled her eyes at Joel and became dead weight in Charlie's arms as he struggled with her, step by step.

Finally, he said, "You're going to have to walk up the rest of the way yourself. I'll push you from behind."

He set her down on her feet two steps above him. She half-turned and planted a round house kick, sending him tipping back down the flight of stairs toward Joel, who moved out of his path.

Joel quickly subdued him, and Catherine picked up the Taurus that had slid down Charlie's pant leg and landed on one of the steps.

The Dade City police, who had arrived along with an ambulance for Sheriff Raspin in response to Joel's 911 call, secured Charlie in the dining room near his mother.

"I told you they'd come someday," Mrs. Crane said to Charlie. "What am I going to do? What should I say?"

"Tell them you raised a psychopath," Catherine snapped.

"All I wanted was to have a normal life with you," Charlie said to Catherine, as he was led out the front door of the Victorian. "I'd have killed to make you my bride."

"It's possible he already did," said Joel, thinking back to the Monroe County case of Meredith Anthony in the parking lot of the tiki bar several weeks earlier. He placed a call to Paz down in the Keys to give the FDLE a heads up on that angle.

Chapter 47
Safe and Secure

Sometime later, back down in the soft, tropical air of the Florida Keys, Joel helped Catherine and Rocky move into his rented cottage in Islamorada. Catherine wanted nothing further to do with the duplex in Marathon, and her landlord had graciously allowed both Catherine and Kate to break their leases without a penalty.

Kate convinced Catherine to come to work with her in Kate's home security business, which had really taken off. It didn't require much convincing, since Catherine had developed a near-obsession with personal safety. They decided to rename the business "Safe and Secure," because Kate had become intrigued with designing floor and wall safes as an additional feature of her electronic monitoring and suite of surveillance options.

"We'll get ourselves a bigger place to live somewhere down here in the Keys after Carmela and I have settled our business," Joel said, as he stood with his arms around Catherine on the dock.

Back inside, Joel took Catherine in his arms and kissed her warmly. She could feel his desire rising as she pressed her hips against his.

"Is it too soon for this?" he asked.

Catherine shook her head and led him to the bed. She pulled off her tee shirt. Joel unhooked her lacy bra, and gently caressed her full breasts.

"Are you sure you're ready for this?" he asked again.

She could feel how hard he was and dug her fingers into his shoulders as he pressed himself against her and kissed her deeply. She slid her hand under the pillow and pulled out one of Charlie's red silk braided cords.

"It depends," she said in a seductive whisper, as she slipped the cord around Joel's left wrist. "Do you want to tie me up, or do you want me to tie you up?"

Shock registered on Joel's face, and then he saw her grin. "Neither one," he laughed. He took the cord and tossed it in the waste basket. "But, if you ever, ever say anything like that in bed again, I might be tempted to at least tie a gag on you!"

Later, Rocky sat on the window ledge in the moonlight, looking serenely out at the ocean while they slept.

THE END

Acknowledgments

First thanks goes to my husband for his patience in enduring my preoccupation with this project over the five or six months of writing and preparing the manuscript.

My sister, Chris Linder, and my brother-in-law, Don Weimer, read the draft and offered valuable suggestions for improving it.

Thanks, also, to the real "Joel" for providing the inspiration to write the novel.

Lastly, thank you to the men and women in law enforcement who strive to keep us safe while working in conditions that, to most of us, are unknowable.

Copyright

This book is a work of fiction. Any references to real people, events, establishments, organizations, or locales are intended only to provide a sense of authenticity and are used fictionally. All other characters, and all incidents and dialogue, are drawn from the author's imagination and are not to be construed as real.

I COULD NEVER FORGET ABOUT YOU. Copyright © 2021 by Leslie J. Linder. All rights reserved under International and Pan-American Copyright Conventions. By payment of the required fees, you have been granted the nonexclusive, nontransferable right to access and read the text of the e-book on screen or the paperback edition. No part of this text may be reproduced, transmitted, downloaded, decompiled, reverse-engineered, or stored in or introduced into any information storage and retrieval system, in any form or by any means, whether electronic or mechanical, now known or hereafter invented, without the express written permission of the author.

Cover design by miblart.com

Also by this Author

An Everglades Romance

Stop Him For Me

The Soldier's Wife

In The House Of The Seventh Messenger

Author Website

www.lesliejanelinder.com

Children's Picture Books by this author writing as "Jane Wesley"

Nicole's Halloween Cat

Nicole's Christmas Kitten

Printed in Dunstable, United Kingdom